M000026180

CHARLIE GLASS
A SHATTERING EXPERIENCE

PART ONE OF THE
CHARLIE GLASS SERIES

AN ORIGINAL NOVEL BY
BUD SELIGSON

Charlie Glass: A Shattering Experience © 2017 Bud Seligson
All rights reserved. No part of this book may be reproduced or transmitted in any form or by any means, electronic or mechanical, including photocopying, recording, or by any information storage and retrieval system, without permission in writing from the Author.

This is a work of fiction! Names, characters, places and incidents are the product of the author's imagination, or are used fictitiously, and any resemblance to actual persons, living or dead, business establishments, events or locale, is strictly un-intended

The following original novel has been copyrighted and registered with the Writer's Guild of America-West under the name of Bud Seligson

Cover Art and Interior design by: Cyrusfiction Productions.

First Edition
ISBN: 978-1-946480-18-7

9018 Balboa Boulevard
Suite #562
Northridge, CA 91325

DEDICATION PAGE

With the exception of doing the research and touring locations, the life of a writer tends to be very solitary and often quite boring. Never more so for me, as when I am working under a deadline. Every year, my wife Diane, puts up with the long hours, and the fact that, even when I am home, I am often mentally elsewhere.

I am a lucky man to be married to such an awesome, and understanding woman.

—BUD SELIGSON

CHAPTER ONE

Los Angeles County Sheriff's Department Sergeant Charlie Glass looked over at his partner, Jack Reed, as he continued to drive down Van Nuys Boulevard.

Charlie was feeling sorry for himself after he had been reassigned yesterday by his station captain as a clear warning to him that his official behavior was once again being brought into question. No more bright lights for a while, no very fine dining at exclusive restaurants, and no more high fashion and good-looking women.

He was thinking that there was nothing on his personal horizon except boring, everyday Sheriff's Department patrols. And nobody was to blame except himself for this current state of affairs. *Myself and those jerks at the top of the Sheriff's Department's command post. They don't appreciate anybody doing the "right thing" when it comes to conflicts with their plans.*

He was thinking that the worst thing about banishment to Van Nuys was the boredom. There weren't enough things going on here to keep his attention. Nothing important, anyway. After all, this was Van Nuys and who cared what was happening here. Nobody he knew gave a damn.

Charlie was driving what the Sheriff's Department called an unmarked car. This car fooled no one in this neighborhood. Everyone knew that two white guys wearing ties in a four-door

Plymouth were the "DTs." The detectives. The Man. They might as well have been in full Sheriff's uniforms and driving an ice-cream truck.

It was a hot and muggy July afternoon, and the streets of Van Nuys were packed with the darker and poorer shaded types of humanity. Right now they were stuck in one of those Southern California traffic jams that occur for no good reason and only seem to end by divine intervention.

Glass's mind floated back to the event two weeks ago that led to his being back on patrol and driving with a new partner down Van Nuys Boulevard.

He had stepped into the hospital about two hours after one of the bank robbers had been rushed there after taking a tremendous fall down some stairs in his attempt to escape from the responding police officers. As lead duty officer, it was Glass's job to get a statement from the man whom the admitting hospital attendant had listed as a John Doe (which meant, in the police ranks, that his actual name was unknown due to a lack of proper identification).

It had turned out that the man's fingerprints gave him up as one Jerome Jackson, a white guy, who lived somewhere in downtown Los Angeles and had a long history of break-ins and armed robbery. Jackson had suffered a tremendous fall down some stairs in his wild attempt to escape from the responding officers.

Glass stood just inside the hospital's emergency room and watched as doctors rushed up and down the corridors, holding onto their examining charts and dashing off to hurried consultations.

Walking into the emergency room's security section, he told the officer on duty that he wanted to speak to the doctor who had admitted the prisoner. The officer looked at Glass's badge, nodded his understanding of what was wanted, and hurried off, returning within a few minutes with a doctor following him.

"I'm Doctor Christopher, sergeant and I am a bit busy at the moment. Kindly make this quick."

"I only need a few seconds of your time, doctor," Detective Second Grade Glass said as he slipped his arm through the doctor's and moved them both off to the side of the corridor. "How is our bank robber Jackson doing?"

"He has a compound fracture of his right elbow and his right shoulder is crushed, as are one or two ribs. There is also some minor internal bleeding going on and he really needs our attention as soon as possible."

"Has he been operated on yet?"

"As you requested, we waited until you got here. He is scheduled for surgery after you complete your initial interview. Right now he is under mild sedation and he must be hurting like hell. As soon as you are done with him, I have ordered him into one of the emergency surgical rooms for immediate attention."

Glass leaned in close to the medical man and whispered quietly. "There is no rush here, doctor. This man is part of a larger gang of bank robbers, and we are hoping to get him to talk to us while the pain has his complete attention. Take care of the good guys first! They should be getting your help long before this son of a bitch."

The doctor wiped his arm across his brow. "I agree," he said, and walked away.

Glass watched him go and took the smile off of his own face as he stepped into the room that held the suspect.

CHAPTER TWO

The robber, Jerome Jackson, lay naked on a gurney with a white sheet neatly folded across his groin. A tube ran from his arm up to a large bottle that hung from a nearby steel pole. His head was propped up on a large white foam-rubber pillow.

Both of his knees were skewed over the side of the gurney: shards of bone protruded from scarlet fissures on his arms and legs. His shoulders were awkwardly positioned, and his eyes were closed.

Glass's sharp eyes noticed that his ears were small and clove-shaped, and he watched quietly as waves of fat rolled over Jackson's hairless body every time he took a breath. He looked more like a circus freak than a professional bank robber and probable killer.

Glass moved up to the hospital trolley. "How do you feel, Jackson?" he asked slowly and clearly.

"How do you think I feel, asshole? They gave me a shot for the fucking pain, but it's wearing off. Call the nurse and tell her I need another shot or something."

Glass moved up to the cream-colored medical cabinet that was against the wall.

"I'd like to give you another shot Jackson, but unfortunately we're running somewhat short on painkillers."

Studying the contents of the medicine cabinet in front of him, Glass opened the clear door and reached inside, removing two plastic bottles of peroxide. He put the bottles down and lightly touched Jackson's leg. Jackson let out an anguished howl.

Glass snatched his hand back. "Oh, I'm sorry, Jackson. I didn't realize that you had an open wound there."

Wincing, Jackson said, "Don't touch, okay? That painkiller is wearing off." His eyes widened with suspicion. " Just who the fuck are you, anyway?"

Glass picked up one of the bottles and unscrewed the cap, which he set down on the nearby table. "I'm Second Grade Sergeant Charles Glass from the Sheriff's Security Division of the Los Angeles County Homicide and Robbery Division."

He leaned over the heavily sweating large man. "I've been a policeman most of my life Mr. Jackson, and during that time I've seen a lot of stupid things. But what you and your partner did this morning is memorable in its stupidity."

He shoved his face even closer to the unhappy man who was looking directly up and into his face. "Did you really think that you could shoot three people and then calmly waltz your ass outside and disappear? We need to talk, and I need to hear from your lips who the brains behind your stupidity are. I need names and any other things that you have rolling around in that fat head of yours, and I need it now."

Jackson turned his head away. "I wanna see my lawyer. I don't have to talk to you. I know my fucking rights."

"Ah, yes. Your fucking rights. Well, I really don't have the time to discuss them with you right now! I have a shooter or two still running around somewhere out there. So I'm going to ask you a few simple questions, and you will give me a few simple answers. Who paid you to shoot up three of our citizens, and why did someone want them shot? I need to know the name of your contact and anything else you would like to tell me."

"FUCK YOU.... I WANNA SEE MY ... "

Glass calmly poured peroxide over the open shard of bone that was protruding from Jackson's leg.

A piercing shriek exploded from the prisoner. Waves of fat heaved over his body as it levitated up off the gurney and he cartwheeled onto the cold floor.

A screaming Jackson rolled from side to side as shards of bone were hitting against the floor and the wheels of the standing gurney.

Two policemen came rushing into the room. Glass calmly shooed them back outside.

Grabbing the other bottle from the tray, he knelt down beside the crying man and began to unscrew the cap right in front of the terrified man's face. "Do you have something you want to tell me, Mr. Jackson?"

Glass then appeared to have second thoughts as he reached under his shirt jacket and slid out his revolver. Gripping the weapon by its barrel, he tapped the butt of the weapon against the bone jutting from one of the thrashing legs.

Thirty-seven minutes later, Glass struck his face out of the cubicle and motioned to one of the nearby standing policemen. "Officer, please see to our guest. He seems to have slipped off the trolley."

CHAPTER THREE

When Charlie stepped out of the hospital's emergency entrance and onto the parking lot, he took a deep breath and a smile rippled across his handsome face. The smells coming from the neighborhood were still those wonderful scents that he remembered so fondly from his early years living not too far south of where he was now standing.

The heavy, sweet smell of Latino and Italian spices filled his head with memories that rushed back to him from the many wonderful years recently gone by. It wasn't very far to the house that he and his sister and their parents lived.

The Glass family had Americanized their name from the Italian immigrant one of Glamonica to Glass when they had come over to the states from Italy in the early 1960s. The four of them all wanted to Americanize everything about themselves, and they all agreed that the name of Glass was about as American as they would ever come up with.

The beginning years for all of them in the Greater Los Angeles area were hard. His father worked double shifts in a factory that made cardboard boxes, and his older sister helped their mother clean people's houses.

They rented a house on the east side of the city that had a small backyard, and the landlord gave them permission to grow a vegetable garden in it. This was an important thing for the family to have, because it continued the family's attachment to the soil that was so very Italian.

This family garden became Charlie's responsibility. He enjoyed working the soil. He liked the smell of the clean earth and the feel of cold dirt under his feet. Charlie felt safe in America as he looked forward to shedding his Italian ways and becoming an American. He wanted to immerse himself in the culture of his new homeland, but that was not to be, at least nor right away.

That part of Los Angeles where the "Glass" family had settled was predominantly Hispanic, and instead of experiencing a bit of the American culture, Charlie found himself living smack in the very center of "Little Mexico." By the time he was eleven years old, he could speak English haltingly. After school he would deliver orders for the local grocery store and made a little pocket money.

Although he was having trouble speaking English, he was able to read and understand the written words quite well. He devoured mystery stories and became the biggest fan of Edgar Rice Burroughs, who not only was famous for his Tarzan of the Apes adventures, but for science fiction stories about the Planet Mars as seen through the eyes of a fellow Earthman who ended up there. The name of this favorite character was John Carter of Mars. In Charlie's opinion, that novel by Edgar Rice Burroughs was the best of all things ever written

John Carter of Mars was written in 1912. It combined otherworldly adventures with elements of classical myths, fast-paced plots and cliff-hanger after unbelievable cliff-hanger. Good, bad or indifferent, this book and this character taught the young and very impressionable Charlie Glass to feel the clanging of a good sword fight and to listen to the cries of damsels in distress and the guttural gesticulations of warriors locked in deadly combat. Charlie's sense of right and wrong came mostly from the epic mold as cast by this John Carter of Mars hero.

In addition to reading every single adventure book that he could get his hands on, Charlie loved to play soccer with his friends and was quite good at the game. Playing soccer developed his powerful legs, and gave him an acute awareness of their strength and fluidity that most American boys his age lacked. Some of the neighborhood's Hispanic kids used to make fun of Charlie's Italian family, who dressed differently and did not speak Spanish to them at all.

,One spring day, Charlie, who was now a developing and powerful fifteen-year-old who had finally mastered the American version of the English language, was working in his garden. He was barefoot and wearing short black pants that his grandfather had sent him from Italy.

He heard snickers from behind him and tensed up, fighting the temptation to turn around and face his tormentors. He completely ignored them, and continued his yard work. But when the laughter grew louder, he did turn around and saw six of the toughest neighborhood kids leaning over the fence in the rear of the yard watching him.

They all started yelling obscene insults at him. "Fucking foreigner! Go back to your stupid country." Four of them leaped over the fence and rushed into the garden, trampling the vegetables, pulling them out of the earth and tossing them all around the yard.

Charlie just stood there watching them and doing nothing about it, with tears of shame burning around his eyes. He suddenly yelled at them to stop and threw his hoe at them.

They hesitated, and stopped what they were doing, as they were all surprised by Charlie's unexpected bravery in defending his garden from them. Then they began to laugh at him standing his ground with adolescent bravado.

Suddenly Charlie rushed at them, targeting the biggest one, a tall burly boy with husky shoulders and big biceps. Charlie could feel the power surging through him as he struck. He arched his right foot up and into the boy's face, knocking out teeth and toppling him onto his knees. Charlie wheeled and smashed his foot into the boy's stomach, splaying him backward onto the ground.

The other boys immediately backed off and away from Charlie's fury as he propelled himself toward them. He kicked another of them in the groin and when he doubled over, he struck out with his foot again and splattered the boy's nose like a crushed tomato. The ferocity of his attack caused the others to break and escape over the fence.

Charlie watched them go, and then turned around and slowly walked into his house, leaving the remaining two bullies rolling around in the dirt.

That evening, when Charlie told his father about what had happened in their back yard, he ruffed his hair and told him that he was proud of him and that he did the right thing to stand up to them. Charlie and his family were never again bothered after that incident in his backyard.

As the years flew by, Charlie became more attuned to his new way of life. He would refuse to speak his native language of Italian unless it was absolutely necessary.

At some point in those early years, he decided that he wanted to become a policeman. Policemen were safe from the taunts of others, and they helped other people; peasants, immigrants, and others who were in need of help.

Charlie Glass's life was now laid out in front of him and he was very excited to get on with it.

CHAPTER FOUR

The years had quickly rolled by, and Charlie Glass, now known as Detective Second Grade Charlie Glass, led the search team that screeched to a stop in front of thirty-four-twenty-nine Main Street, just north of downtown Los Angeles.

The robbed and looted store was going to be taken apart by Glass's "Special Team Security Robbery Division." Electrical fixtures and plates were removed from the wall and ceilings. Moldings were pried from their baseboards. Floor coverings were taken up, rugs and furniture were vacuumed and their fibers were carefully deposited into plastic evidence bags. All the papers were removed from drawers and cabinets, and then indexed and cross-referenced. Photographs were taken and fingerprints were lifted.

Detective Glass moved about the rooms, supervising the operations, his hands carefully kept behind his back so as not to touch anything. He watched as special plastic bags were placed over the hands and tied around the wrists of the deceased in order to preserve any scrapings that might be wedged under the nails or in the crevices of each hand.

Outside the store, Security Division investigators moved up and down the street, canvassing for witnesses. An eyewitness account was the most valuable part of the early working of any case. Several uniformed officers maintained a security zone in front of the shop as they chased away the curious passersby. Nearby shopkeepers were grumbling that they were losing business with all the police activity going on around them They were ignored, and the detailed investigation continued.

Glass's direct superior, Lieutenant Ganz, appeared in the doorway with two folders under his arm. He looked a lot like a very worried accountant, an impression reinforced by his prematurely graying hair. "Here are the files on the dead officers," he said handing them to Glass.

Looking around the store for some quiet place and finding none, Glass went out into the street, using the folders to shield his face from the strong sunlight, and crossed the street to his car. It was parked half-up on the narrow sidewalk, blocking the front of a clothing store, whose owner was locked in a heated discussion with a nearby uniformed policeman.

Glass slid into the rear seat of the car, and was just opening up one of the files, when a knock on the car's roof interrupted him.

"Yes?" Glass said to one of the uniformed policemen.

"We need you inside, sir! We've found something."

Detective Second Grade Charlie Glass got out of the car and returned to the cool, dark interior of the storefront.

CHAPTER FIVE

Even though it was his regular day off, Charlie, as usual, was doing something connected with one of his cases on his own time.

On this special day, we find him in Westwood, California, the location of the wonderful west side campus of the University of California–Los Angeles.

He was killing some time while waiting for a call from one of his undercover guys, who was following up on the lead that he had received yesterday on the double murder case of the two policemen in downtown Los Angeles.

He had wandered into a small coffee shop on Westwood Boulevard and was delivered his coffee and sweet roll by a very attractive waitress who kept glancing his way.

Charlie disconnected the earphone as he told his contact that he was on his way. He checked his watch, took one last slip of his coffee, folded the local newspaper and stood up.

The ever-watchful waitress slowly walked over to Charlie and placed his bill on the end of the small table. She looked admiringly at him as she said, "Nice pants. Great butt." Still wearing her wonderful smile, the waitress said in a very soft voice, "You should know that I have a specific copyright on that saying."

Charlie glanced down at her and gave her one of his best smiles. He was very serious as he answered her attempt at humor. "I'll just bet that you don't." Pausing to give serious thought to the matter, Charlie said with a smile in his voice, "I'll bite. What do you think it's worth if I ever want to use those words?"

Without any hesitation, she replied, "Dinner at a nice restaurant." Seeing the smile on Charlie's face, she quickly added, "I want you to know that I am really embarrassed about this whole conversation! I"ve never been this aggressive before."

Continuing to wear his best smile, Charlie takes his phone out of his shirt pocket and hands it to the surprised waitress.

"Please hold on to this for me. I'll give you a call the first moment I can. Of course I already know this telephone number, but right now I'm running a few minutes late for a very important meeting. My name is Charles Glass, and I would be very pleased to meet you if only I knew your name."

"My friends call me Lori! Lori Hampton! I'm going to look forward to your call, Charles Glass. But right now you had better get going to that important meeting."

One last smile passed between them as Charlie leaves the cafe with his mind whirling.

Lori Hampton was a very attractive young lady! He would judge her to be in her middle twenties, and she probably was working as a waitress until her agent called her. Everyone in Los Angeles had an agent.

He suspected that she was another wannabe actress, but he was thinking about her in a completely different way. She was very attractive and seemed to have a great personality. She just might be the perfect lady for him to get to know better. He was excited about his chance meeting with her.

Another good thing in Lori's favor was that she must be living not too far away, since she was working in Westwood. It would be a lot easier to court her and bed her down at his leisure here in Los Angeles.

Charlie continued to smile as he hustled to his meeting place.

CHAPTER SIX

The wind was barely strong enough to make a feeble effort at moving the leaves on the trees that lined the long driveway in front of the restaurant. Charlie had just given the parking attendant a twenty-dollar tip as he took the keys from him, while carefully helping Lori Hampton into the passenger seat of his newly purchased Mercedes.

While they were buckling up with the oversized seat belts, Lori had turned to him and asked him to tell her something about this exceptional-looking car. She said that she knew that it was one of a kind, and that she was sure that there was an interesting history connected to it.

As he slowly pulled out of the restaurant's circular driveway, Charlie's mind was flashing back to last week, when he had been out looking for something new and different in a high-end car. He was in the showroom of the Mercedes dealership on Wilshire Boulevard in Beverly Hills, when he saw three men pushing something very black and very interesting onto the showroom floor.

"What is that one coming in all about?" he asked the salesman.

"Good question, sir! That is a specially made Mercedes model called an E-55. It is first cousin to the usual E4-30 that you are probably familiar with. This E-55 has been specially modified, and the exterior finish is something new in a special metallic black with parchment-leather upholstery."

"I can tell that it's something interesting. Tell me the story on this car. I just might be interested if it's really different and the price is right."

The salesman went over to a nearby desk, and after moving a few papers around, he pulled out a red folder. He went over to a copy machine that was in the far comer of the showroom, and made two copies of the report. He then went back to the desk and returned the file into the drawer. Charlie was already sitting in the E-55's driver's seat, and the salesman opened up the passenger door and sat down with a pleased expression on his face.

Charlie assumed that James, the salesman, enjoyed talking about something different from the ordinary cars that passed through the showroom. And it was not every day that he could sit down and discuss something as interesting as the E-55.

Charlie followed him with his eyes on his copy of the paperwork as James read out loud.

"This car is one of a kind; it is very much out of the ordinary! It has a five-and-a-half-liter V-9 engine that is more powerful than any other Mercedes that has ever been built. It has been brought up to three hundred fifty-four horsepower, with a specially built transmission to make sure that it can easily handle all that power. The body itself has been lowered, and the suspension system has upgraded shock absorbers, anti-roll bars and two sets of very special springs. It has eighteen-inch wheels, special-rated over-sized tires and extremely heavy-duty brakes."

Charlie, who was listening to every word that was being said, was having trouble holding back his emotions, and he told himself to calm down.

James was still talking....

"The windows are tinted darkly enough to make the various occupants within the car completely unrecognizable, and after it arrived in the United States, we sent it out to a specialist to be lightly armored!

"What exactly do you mean when you say, "lightly armored?" Charlie asked.

James opened up his passenger side door, pressed a button and the window rolled down half-way. "As you can easily see, the side glass is a lot thicker than the standard window glass. It is a full one-half-inch thick, which is unheard of. And the roof, all the door panels and the floor pan have all been reinforced with extremely light-weight but very tough materials like Kevlar. The car will repel small-weapons fire, even heavy machine-gun fire, but it won't, of course, be able to stop a bazooka or a large landmine. You would need the fully armored version for that level of protection."

The salesman went on: "You have sport seats and special trim all the way around, and there is also a specially concealed radar scrambler under the dashboard," he said, as he looked around to see if anyone else was listening to their conversation.

"I love the car. What's your asking price?"

"Actually, this car doesn't belong to this agency," the salesman replied in a quiet voice. "It's the property of the widow of a former client of ours, a South American gentleman."

"And why is she a widow?" Charlie asked with a big smile on his handsome face.

"The car was delivered a few days too late to serve the purpose for which the South American gentleman intended it."

"You mean he was in another car when …"

"When he needed the extra protection that this car would have afforded him."

"And tell me James, how much does the sad widow want for the car?"

"Something in the neighborhood of $_____."

He named a figure and Charlie touched his inside jacket pocket to make sure that he had his checkbook with him. "Ask the widow if she will accept my offer of $_____." Charlie named a number. "And please tell her that it will be my one and only offer."

"Let me make a telephone call," the salesman said. He went to his desk and picked up the telephone.

CHAPTER SEVEN

Charlie snapped back to reality and remembered that the beautiful Lori had just asked him a question about his fabulous new car.

"To answer your question, Lori, I must confess that I really don't know too much about the original owner. I was told that he had recently passed away, and the family had no use for such a big car without him. I happened to be at the right place at the right time, and now this baby belongs to me! I'm glad you like it."

While they were talking, Charlie was driving down Wilshire Boulevard, which took them from Beverly Hills into the Westwood area of Los Angeles. This area was built around the UCLA campus, where Charlie had purchased an apartment in one of the many high-rise buildings that were everywhere in the West Los Angeles/Westwood area.

The Mercedes was given to the doorman as Charlie led the way into the elevator which took them up to the twenty-fifth floor.

There was no hesitation on Lori's part going with him to his apartment. She was very attracted to the interesting Charlie Glass, and if it led to sleeping with him on the first date, she really did not care. Her idea was to simply do things so well that she would overshadow the other women that she knew he had in his bachelor's life style. It wasn't often that she met such a successful, good-looking and well-educated guy, and she was going for the brass ring, no matter what!

It was drilled into her head that good girls did not sleep with their dates until at least the third date, but wasn't this really the second time they were together? The first one being at the restaurant where they first met last week.

The hell with it, she thought. She was prepared to go all the way if she had to. The worst that she could do was have the great sex that she knew was in front of her. Where was the downside, and just what did she have to lose?

And so, with a light spirit and a good attitude, she stepped into his apartment on the twenty-fifth floor that looked down upon the entire world.

The door was unlocked. Lori stepped into the large entryway and was immediately enchanted.

The entryway led them into a huge room off to the left of the foyer entrance, a study or an office of some sort. There was a beautiful and quite massive desk that seemed to be carved out of one single piece of unstained wood. It dominated the room with its aged handles and trim that went around the entire desk. A multicolored greenish blotter lay precisely centered on the desk with a set of four differently colored marking pens lying there in a neat row.

The walls were surrounded with rich wooden shelves that groaned with the weight of books, drums, masks and old weaponry that looked as if they had all come from very exotic lands.

Lori was immediately attracted by a wall space between the shelves, occupied by brightly colored shields fronted by two crossed swords. One set was an ancient English kite-shield holding another two crossed swords, and the other was an African Zulu buffalo-hide shield with scimitars.

Lori knew that museums would jump at the chance if they could only get their hands on a collection half this rich and so interestingly varied.

Charlie led her further into the apartment, showing her the

wealthy splendor of hardwood floors and custom carved wood statues and working fountains, and several real-looking suits of armor.

They spent over an hour looking at several original paintings that added a great deal of class and bright colors to the walls. One of the ones she knew was an original Van Gogh. It was most impressive, and Lori wondered just what it was that Charlie Glass did for a living that allowed him to live in the warm and wonderful world that seemed to surround him.

Despite trying not to be, Lori realized that she was extremely curious as to just who and what he really was. He had to be much more than most men his age, just to justify all the things she saw and all the things. she was slowly finding out about this mysterious man. She confirmed her earlier resolve to herself, that no matter what was required of her this evening, she was going to be okay with it.

They ended up standing with drinks in hand in front of the dining room's clear glass window that looked down on the Westwood campus of the University. The city lights from that vantage point were overwhelming.

The two of them seemed perfectly content and quite happy to be with each other, as they continued to stand there holding hands and just looking out into the distance. It was not long until Charlie's fingers slid carefully around her soft neck, as he tenderly kissed her with a very slow, sexy and lingering kiss.

Lori sighed deeply and returned his kiss, as she wrapped her arms around this great hunk of masculinity. She felt herself simply unable to resist the sweet, hot warmth of his tongue against hers. The feel of his hands running over her back as he held her close, seemed so right. It felt good to have him touch her as she felt the heat of his body coming through to her.

Suddenly, they were deeply kissing each other, drinking in a deep intensity that seemed so very special.

Lori felt like she would simply die if she did not have more of him. Her tongue stroked his in return.

He twined his long fingers into her hair, tugging away the band holding it at the nape of her neck. He continued to angle her mouth to his, taking more of her, and it was still not enough for him.

She leaned firmly into him and felt the thick ridge of his erection melding to her moving hips.

"You feel good," he murmured, "so damn good." Charlie wrapped his arms around her and pulled her closer, twining his fingers in her silky hair. He inhaled the familiar scent of roses that was so much this woman. It was a wonderful sensation. With his mouth held gently over hers, his tongue continued to caress her, in long, languid strokes that had them both moaning with the contact, with the connection, with the sudden burning between them.

Seconds ticked by and they were still satisfied just kissing, softly and tenderly.

CHAPTER EIGHT

Charlie hardly remembered how his shirt, pants and shoes came off, but he remembered everything about undressing Lori Hampton. He roughly pulled her top upward and over her head, and quickly but carefully, unhooked her nicely overflowing bra and unzipped her skirt.

Lori casually tossed her clothing aside as Charlie quickly filled his hands with her high, full breasts and stroked her plump pink nipples. He gently pressed her back against the nearest wall, his gaze devouring her almost naked body, while she helped remove whatever jewelry she still had on. She left on her dark stockings, garter belt, and panties.

She kicked aside her accumulated clothing as Charlie went down to his knees in front of her. His hands quickly went to her hips and his lips slid down to her flat stomach.

"Finally," he breathed out. "I've been looking forward to this all evening."

He slid his hands delicately to her smooth backside, while he bent his head, brushing his lips over her hips, trailing kisses over to her mid-section, widening the space between her thighs and kissing her very slowly. He explored the intimate vee of her body, his fingers teasing the slick wet heat of her sexual arousal that he had felt coming on.

He suddenly stood up and scooped her off of her feet as easily as if she were a mere child, and headed to the far end of the apartment toward his bedroom.

Moonlight was spilling into the large master bedroom as Charlie carefully deposited her back in the center of the huge bed. He thoughtfully placed an oversized pillow beneath her head to ensure her comfort.

Charlie pressed his lips to hers and slid his tongue carefully into her mouth once again as the sweetness of her completely filled his senses. He tasted her with his eyes, seeking the flavor of her openness, her willingness and possibly the beginning of her love.

His eager hands roamed freely over her willing body, and she shivered with pleasant chills that were running up and down her spine. He palmed her breasts once again, teasing her nipples and plucking them into tight little peaks.

Lori gently wrapped her hand around the base of his erection, and Charlie could actually feel himself thicken with her touch and the anticipation of what was yet to come. She guided him to the wet slick center of her body, and she felt him shaking with his suddenly urgent need. He seemed to be trying to resist pushing into her on his own, rather than waiting for her to take him there.

She easily pressed his throbbing shaft inside her, as she slid down the length of him, taking him in all at once.

Charlie was thinking about how hot and tight she was, and how she was so wet for him and she felt ever so good! Raw hunger rose inside him as he moaned loudly while pressing her down deeply into the softness of the bed, and lifted her hips to allow him to smoothly thrust himself inside of her.

Her body tightened around his throbbing erection as she took him hard and deep inside of her. Her fingers were in his hair, and their soft touches sent shivers up and down his spine. He just loved her kisses, those delicate, sweet kisses that could be so wild and wicked and yet at the same time, so soft and feminine!

Lori seemed to be everything that he wanted her to be. Could she be the one that he was searching for all these years?

He was still hungry for her as she seemed to be for him and that was wonderful. It was in their every move, in their every touch, in their every groan of pleasure. If they could have melted into each other and become one, they would have done just that at that moment.

Lori leaned back as Charlie's hands settled on her flat stomach, pumping himself into her, as she allowed him to ride her in their erotic dance. Her beautiful breasts swayed with the rhythm of their bodies, and her nipples seemed to be calling for his mouth once again. She spiked her fingers again through his hair with her moans turning into sexy little pants of pleasure that were driving her wild.

Charlie knew that he was coming to the end of his ability to hold back from the final bursting of his manhood into her welcoming body, and he pushed and thrust with the final moments of the glorious pleasure that she was giving him.

"Yes, Charlie," she moaned, burying her face in his neck. "So … good … Charlie."

With his name on her lips, asking him to pleasure her for the last time, he was driven over the edge and could not hold himself back any longer.

For the two of them, almost in perfect timing, the room disappeared, and the present moment also disappeared, because there was only the flush of completion to the wonderful sex act that they shared. As they both came to final completion, the two of them just collapsed into each-others' arms and laid there, unable to move even if they wanted to. For long seconds, they clung to one another, skin damp and breathing heavy.

"I love you, Charlie. I really do. I never felt something like this before."

And with her words bouncing around inside his head, he held her close and softly kissed her lips as the two of them fell into a deep and most pleasant sleep.

CHAPTER NINE

The next morning, Sheriff's Detective Second Grade Charlie Glass arrived at work at the squad room in Police Headquarters at 9:30 AM, half an hour early. Inspector Roberto Chanchez was sitting at Charlie's desk waiting for him.

"There's been a murder," Chanchez announced. "Two of them, in fact, and I need your help, Charlie."

"Inspector, unless you have something really special here, I'm up to my eyeballs on the robbery and double cop killing on the other side of downtown," Charlie answered. "Regular murder cases, unless there is something unusual about them, are handled by the Homicide Division and not by my robbery guys, and I'm sure that you know this. Why am I getting the feeling that I'm not going to like what you're about to tell me?"

"You're right about that. One of the victims is Kathy Barnes. Does that name ring a bell?"

"Kathy Barnes? Who's she?"

"The married daughter of John Ganz."

"Uh-oh. The speaker of the city council, that John Ganz?"

"The very same. Her body and the body of a man not known to be her husband were found in a lovers' lane up on Mulholland Drive a few hours ago. The male was executed straight out, one bullet to the back of the head. This is bad, but the girl got it much worse. She was raped, tortured, and then beaten to death. Might be some kind of sadistic bondage thing according to the first report that just came in," the Inspector mumbled.

"Are you assigning me to this murder case, Inspector? If so I'll have to turn over the case I'm working on to my second-in-command and clear the deck."

"Yep, this one is all yours, and your orders are to report to Captain Crewe at two o'clock this afternoon. He will fill you in on the case. I'm sorry to do this to you, Charlie, but this is going to be a political hot cake, and there is no one else that I want on the case but you. Clear your cases and report to the captain forthwith."

§

Senior Captain Crewe was on speakerphone, sitting back in his chair with his feet up on his ornate desk when Detective Glass entered his large office on the fourteenth floor of the Criminal Justice Building on Spring Street in Central Los Angeles. Although he was ten years older than Charlie, the two of them appeared to be about the same age.

It was the captain's confident attitude, his great outgoing personality, his full head of straight, jet-black hair and his dimples that made him look under forty. People liked the captain minutes after just meeting him for the first time, and he was always thought of as "one of the good old boys" in the department.

Captain Crewe closed his speakerphone conversation with a "Thanks a lot, Tommy! I won't forget that I owe you one for this favor." Then he hung up, took his feet off the desk and turned his attention to Charlie Glass. "Whatcha been up to, Charlie?"

"Been busy, Captain, but not really killing myself," Glass answered the big boss.

"I'm glad you're not being overworked Charlie, because I'm giving you this Barnes case. I really need your help on this case. I'm under a lot of pressure from the Big Guy upstairs, and I need one of your special miracles here. I'm giving you first position on this one. This is going to be a goddamned hot one as soon as the press catches the names."

"You do know, Captain, that I haven't worked a specific homicide case in years? But I don't mind your assigning me to it. As always, I'll do my best for you, sir."

Glass was lying and the captain knew that he was lying, but it was expected of Glass to say the things he was saying to keep things light and moving along in the right direction.

"What does the press know so far?"

"As usual, they probably know quite a bit already, but what they don't know yet is that one of the victims is the Barnes girl. The pressure on this case won't happen until they find out who the female was. And then the game will begin in earnest."

"Who was the other victim?"

"The guy? We don't know yet! The lab boys took his prints, so we should know soon. The killer took his wallet, so we don't have identification yet. I'm just hoping he's not the son of some other big shot from our local area. We don't need a double dose of these big-time players screaming at us on this one.

CHAPTER TEN

Glass had a hard time locating the crime scene. He cruised around on Mulholland Drive where it touched Coldwater Canyon heading over from the San Fernando Valley toward Laurel and the central city of L.A. After going in circles for a while, he got lucky as a police car from one of the local precinct's passed him by and he was able to follow it.

Glass saw the driver, a female cop, eye him in her rearview mirror, and then her male partner turned around in his seat to get a quick look at him. They turned off the road, across a flat roadway and onto the edge of a wooded area surrounded by a narrow dirt trail about fifty yards deep before it ended. The road was blocked by a crime scene unit's van, along with a half a dozen other cars.

As he got out of his car, Glass noted a few radio-dispatched cars, some unmarked detective cars, and a morgue wagon. The two uniformed cops he had followed to the crime scene got out of their car and waited for him to walk up to them.

Charlie guessed that both officers were in their early thirties and must have been on the job for a while. The thick row of in-service medals around their official badges, told him that they hadn't spent their time idly. They were sharp cops, and it later turned out that his first impression was correct.

The male was the serious one on the team. He was dark

and handsome and reminded Charlie of Rudolph Valentino, the movie star.

Opposites sometimes do attract, and they obviously did in this case with the police partners. She was not so good looking, but she was all smiles as she walked up to him and extended her hand. "Are you going to be working this case, Detective Glass, she asked?"

Glass did not know either of the two officers but was not surprised at his being recognized. "Yes, I am."

"Then you're gonna want to talk to us. We discovered the crime scene and the bodies .

What a good piece of luck it was following the two cops. He would have had to look them up later on. He would talk to them now and get some insider information before he looked at the crime scene. Charlie was excited that he was getting started in the best possible way.

While Officer Ryan told him how they had found the bodies, Charlie noticed that his partner was taking a dozen or so paper cups filled with coffee from the back seat of their patrol car. This told Charlie that he would be walking right into a full-blown crime scene that had definitely been in place for a while.

Charlie stopped Ryan from telling his story when he asked him what officials were here already.

"Our captain, our sergeant and another full team from the 47th Street Station. There's also a Lieutenant from the Homicide Squad who came out first after we reported the bodies." Ryan was sorry but he could not remember any more of the names. "Then there were six officers from the local crime scene unit, and a crew from Emergency Services." And the last one that he remembered was the doctor who took the first call and officially opened up the crime scene.

Charlie spent the next ten minutes asking about their discovery of the bodies and how it all came about.

The female partner started to finish up the narrative, but first she added that he should really talk to the sergeant who was down there on the scene. She said that he was a real old-timer with lots of old-time ways, but he really knew how to get the job done.

Charlie had worked with many of the older semi-retired investigators before, and he knew that they all played everything by the rule books. They would follow the rules exactly as they were written. Run afoul of them by breaking the traditional way of going through things, and they would be hell on wheels as they fought you every inch of the way if they thought you were going in the wrong direction. Charlie learned to let them take the lead in all their specialties, and he would get the best results for any problems that popped up. He knew to whom he could turn to for any deep diggings that were always necessary on a case like this one promised to be.

His briefing by the two patrol officers was worth their weight in gold—and he told them so. He saw them each stand up straighter and taller as he let them know the value he attached to them. He told them that they would be called upon to help him gather some of the vital details that would be needed to get the investigation going.

He told them he would be calling their station to request a transfer from there over to his Homicide Division. He told them to mention to their sergeant that he would be sending the request over. The officers had nothing but smiles for him from that time on.

"Rudolph Valentino' continued with his narrative after Charlie led him into it with an important question. "Officer, do you know or believe that this spot has been used as a lovers' lane before this incident?"

"Sometimes," came the answer. "But the lovers are always gone by the time we get here in the early morning. We always find empty beer cans, wine bottles, pizza boxes and things like that.

We like to keep our patrol areas tidy so we always clean up after these slobs."

Charlie was thinking that this might be a big break for the investigation. Anything found here after the area was cleaned up the night before would have had to include evidence from the actual crime that followed the officers' clean-up of the area. Their habit of cleaning up by his newly highly prized investigating cops could possibly turn something up that was left by the killer or killers.

There was one last thing that he had to ask the eager-to-please officers before he let them go. He said in a casual voice, "I see that you went out for coffee for everyone who is down there at the crime scene. Are there any reporters here that I should be aware of, and if so, how much of what you saw and reported do they know?"

The female cop responded that they really had no way of knowing what the two reporters were told so far on the case, but just looking at the crime scene told its own story. She suggested that he follow them down the path leading to the area in question.

Charlie thanked them for the briefings and told them that they would be hearing from him in a day or two.

The two officers nodded an acknowledgement and led the way down the trail to the crime scene, where tape was stretched across a large area.

CHAPTER ELEVEN

John Smith of the *Daily News* and Sam Mesa of the *Los Angeles Times* were there, talking to each other and looking bored. They were both in their mid-forties, but the stress of their jobs hadn't gotten to them. They each had a full head of dark hair with little if any gray, and they both looked as if they did not have a single care in the world.

Charlie had known both men for many years and counted them as friends. They were two good guys who had been around the crime scene long enough to know that breaking a confidence meant burning out an inside source forever, and so they were known to keep their ideas to themselves until they were told that it was the right time to release their stories. There was no need to assign a cop to the crime-scene tape to keep them at bay. They would wait for the official statement, and then, with the proper permission, they would get to take some pictures.

Smith and Mesa's casual and unexcited demeanor told Charlie that they had obviously not been given the female victim's name. It looked like they both considered this crime scene to be just another routine double murder and this was no big thing to them.

That all changed the moment they saw Detective Sergeant Second Grade Charlie Glass arrive on the scene. Both reporters quickly realized that there was something up here that they both had not been aware of. Something extraordinary must have happened here, and they were both pleased that they seemed to be in the right spot at the right time,

"Are you going to talk to us, Charlie?" Smith asked with a serious look on his face.

"Don't know much yet, but I'll give you what I know."

Smith and Mesa each grabbed a coffee container from the female cop who was serving. She wisely stepped out of hearing range when she saw that Charlie was going to engage the two reporters into a conversation.

Charlie noted that the two cops took themselves away from himself and the two reporters. They were wise and experienced examples of the best of the Los Angeles Sheriff's Department. He knew that he would be able to count on them as the case progressed.

"You able to talk to us now about this case, Charlie?" Smith asked him again.

"Yep, I can definitely talk to you! I just got assigned to it by headquarters and I'm not up to speed yet, but I soon will be."

"Are you officially transferred into the Homicide Division for this case?"

"No, I'm not. I'm just helping out! I'm just on loan here from my usual Major Case and Robbery Division."

"So, this must be some sort of special murder to get you down here with the rest of us."

"Yeah, it's turning out to be a special murder case, and a very delicate one at that."

"Why's that, Charlie?" Mesa asked. "Does it have to do with who the identified female victim is?"

"You got it right, Mesa. It's about who the victims are."

"As I understand it Charlie, you've only got one of them identified so far, and that one is the female. So we all can assume that so far the person of interest in this double whammy is the female. Do I get this right, Charlie?"

"You got that right, Mesa. This is going to be one hell of a story before it's over! I'm sure that you and all of your pals are going to put a lot of heat on me before it's finished, so let's cut this interview short and let me get down there and see what's happening. Just stay around so I can talk to you guys on my way out. I'll send one of the coffee cops over to you to fill you in on the names and stuff that have turned up so far. I'll give you more later, when I get going on the case. Nice to see you both."

As he ducked under the tape, he looked back and saw that both men were on their cell phones calling their editors to suggest that they send some photographers out to the top of Mulholland Drive as soon as possible. Something big was breaking, and they wanted the exclusive coverage. Charlie knew that the three-ring-circus was coming and all hell was about to break loose.

The female victim's BMW was still parked at the top end of the dirt trail as Charlie walked past it. Fellow Detective Joe Wahl was busy dusting the passenger door handles of the car, while several other uniformed policemen watched and sipped at their coffee.

Charlie stopped for a moment to listen to the running commentary Detective Wahl was giving as he worked. He was explaining his craft to all who cared to listen. The cops surrounding him looked bored, which told Charlie that they had been standing there too long.

"I don't have much for you right now, Detective Glass, but I can tell you one thing for sure," Detective Wahl was saying. "This is one of the cleanest crime scenes that I have seen in a long time. The killer was either really smart or really careful or perhaps a little of both. I'm not getting much of anything that he left behind."

Wahl' words were a real disappointment to Charlie. If Wahl couldn't find anything, then nobody else would. This was starting to look like a real tough one.

Charlie stopped for a moment to take in the terrific view that was surrounding him. This really was a great spot for a lovers' lane! It was just about on top of Mulholland Drive and if you looked back toward the north, you saw the bright lights of the spread out San Fernando Valley, and if you turned in a half circle and looked directly south, you were looking down at central Los Angeles and the Hollywood area, winking and blinking at you in all of their glittering glory.

CHAPTER TWELVE

Charlie continued to stand there quietly as he watched Detective Joe Wahl, who was the ultimate investigator when it came to physical evidence. Lying on the ground next to the very detailed Wahl were many thick evidence bottles and containers that he was using to hold the various items that he was gathering from the bloody scene.

Over the years Charlie had learned to respect and to like the heavyset, rough-speaking and very detailed inspector as he went about his work. If Detective Wahl told you that something he found was available as evidence, then his discovery was always accurate and would hold up well in the prosecution of a case in the criminal court system. He could be quite charming as well as being extremely accurate. He would present his evidence from a crime scene with such clarity and precision that the big brass of the Sheriff's Department always wanted Wahl to be the first one out there. His reputation was spotless and unquestionable. If this detective told you that something was this way or that way, you could rely on it being exactly so.

As he watched Wahl going about doing whatever it was that he was doing, Charlie became aware of his own personal high emotions that always ran rampant through him when he visited a crime scene for the first time. This one especially gave him cause for concern, as it was a bloody double homicide that would be a real tough case with all the publicity that was sure to follow, and it would be dogging him every foot of the way.

He was thinking seriously about bringing over one of the female detectives to handle the press for him and to take the day-to-day load off his back of having to answer the repetitive questions that would keep coming and coming. He was aware that his own feelings of grief and anger that murder always generated in him would soon pass as he intellectually got into the case. The excitement of the chase always kept his mind clear.

One of his favorite saying in the whole world came from the fictional character Sherlock Holmes, whose ability to solve a crime was never topped by any detective, real or fictional. Sir Arthur Conan Doyle's complete collection of Sherlock Holmes mysteries were in his private collection at home in his apartment on Wilshire Boulevard. The saying that he always wanted to use, was always right at his fingertips, "Let us go, Watson. The game is afoot!"

The problem here was that there was no Doctor Watson to assist his role of Sherlock Holmes, and Charlie, who was well aware of his limitations, tried to set his personal emotions aside as he got himself involved in this newly assigned case. It was his job to find the son of a bitch who took the lives of two vibrant and living persons who were just out there in the world living their lives as best they could, and deserved better than the terrible things that were done to them.

§

When Detective Wahl finally pulled off his gloves and set down the few items that he had been carrying, Charlie walked over to him, planning to engage him in a conversation.

"Hey Wahl, any private thoughts that you could share with me?" he said with a big smile on his face. "I need to get up to speed on this one, and there is no one better than you to catch me up!"

The detective grinned at Charlie as he absorbed the compliment. "I think I have it pretty well figured out, and if you would like, let's walk through it and see if you agree with some of my conclusions.

A pleased Charlie Glass followed Detective Wahl for a short distance, going somewhat deeper into the wooded area off of the Mulholland Highway Roadway, until they finally stopped beside a fallen tree that blocked their path.

"This is where the killer waited for his victims to arrive. It looks like he just sat here on this tree for quite a while, just calmly waiting."

Wahl got down on his hands and knees, and Charlie quickly followed him down as Detective Wahl pointed to some cigarette ashes intermingled with the dead leaves. "No way of telling how many smokes he had, but he was careful, and he took his butts with him. He left nothing else to show that he was ever here, and it shows us that the killer did not know Kathy and her friend, who just happened to be the first to arrive at the scene.

"The killer was here waiting for them as targets of opportunity! He must have just walked into the area and over to the tree, and when he was done with everything, he just seemed to walk away and disappear. He probably walked a long way to where he must have left his getaway vehicle. The only clue that all of this left us is that we can safely assume that he had to be from around here in order to have known about this lovers' lane.

"After his victims arrived, he must have waited a few minutes longer while they went at it in the car. Her boyfriend gets his pants down, but we don't know what state of dress or undress she was in because none of her clothing was found in the car."

Charlie stared at the ground, searching for something that the killer might have left behind, but Joe Wahl was right. There was nothing but ashes. No footprints, no paper, nothing but cigarette butts.

"Are you ready for me to go on, Charlie?" asked Detective Wahl as he saw him looking around at the surrounding area.

Both men got back to their feet, and Charlie followed the Inspector back to the BMW.

"The killer walks over here on the driver's side of the front doors, and fires one shot through the closed window, killing the male victim instantly. It was a clean and clear shot, and that shows us that the shooter was familiar with his weapon."

"Was there any trace of the bullet?"

"No, but I would bet that he used an automatic weapon and held the gun in a paper bag to catch the ejected cartridge when he fired. I'm also betting that when the lab boys pull the slug out of the victim's head, they're going to find paper residue burned into it from the bag."

Charlie was thinking something very important to himself at that moment. *Were they dealing with a serial killer here?* Some of the things that Detective Wahl was describing here sounded sort of familiar.

"What kind of gun do you think he was using?"

"If I had to guess, I'd say a .380 Colt Commander."

Charlie waited for more facts from Detective Wahl to justify some random thoughts that were popping in and out of his head. He could not quite put his finger on anything, but there was an itch here that he could not scratch. He decided to hold his thoughts close to his vest and wait for things to move further along. "What happened next?"

"The boyfriend never saw it coming, but whatever she was doing at that moment, Kathy did. After the shot, she must have had the presence of mind and was smart enough to open her side door and jump out of the car and run. But she wasn't fast enough and didn't get very far."

Charlie followed Detective Wahl around the car to the passenger side of the front door and followed him again back into the woods.

"This is where he caught her," the detective said, pointing to the ground a few yards ahead of where they were walking. He tackled her from behind and brought her down, face first. I found several things here. There was some blood on several of the leaves here, presumably Kathy's, so he must have smacked her to bring her under control, and I am assuming that he hit her on the side of her head with his gun because there is a nasty lump on her head.

"I also found this where we are now standing." He unfolded a handkerchief to reveal a thin gold hoop earing with a small blood smear on it.

"Which side of her head is the lump on?" Charlie asked.

"The right side."

"It doesn't look like there was much of a struggle here. So I would say that he hit her from behind when she was on the ground after he had tackled her, and if so then he would have been holding the gun in his right hand."

"That is my thinking too."

"So we're looking for a right-handed killer, but that does not help us much."

"To continue with my narrative, I believe that after he hit her and had her under complete control, that he dragged her over here. That is evident by the drag marks on the ground."

Charlie followed him to a large tree growing at the very edge of the precipice.

"Be very careful how you walk here, but I want you to look at the other side of this tree."

Charlie held onto the trunk of the tree and swung his upper body away so that he could easily see that side of the thick tree trunk.

It was easy to see that there were several recently scarred cuts evident on the far side, some of which were deeply grooved and some which were lightly scratched into the soft surface. One of the deeply scarred scratches was up from the bottom base of the tree, and the other was higher up, possibly about five feet high

Detective Wahl quietly said, "It looks like he tied her with chains of some sort, and they must have been around her neck and her ankles because that would correspond with someone who stood about five foot one or two in her bare feet."

CHAPTER THIRTEEN

"How tall was Kathy?"

"I'm only guessing here. I believe she was around five foot two or three."

"Looks like he did tie her to the tree at her neck and at her ankles as you said. I also agree that he must have used some sort of chain to make those heavy-duty kinds of marks!"

Detective Wahl commented that the killer might have used a couple of chain dog-leashes, but it was the way he tied her that struck him as unusual. He continued, "He must have used two sets of handcuffs. The first set went on each wrist and he must have backed her up against the side of the tree with a chain tied around her neck to secure her. Then we have to assume that he stretched her cuffed hands back, ran the chain through the cuffs and secured everything on the back side of the tree and away from where she could get at anything. He must have gagged her to prevent her from making any loud noises.

"The trail leading from that tree back to where I showed you that spot where he was sitting and smoking is extremely worn down. The grass that was underfoot is just about all gone, which shows us that he must have gotten up several times from where he was sitting to check on Kathy. While he was having his smokes, he probably was waiting to see if anyone else would be showing up. If anyone else came by he either would have left or attacked the new arrivals as well. But Kathy was not that lucky, and obviously no one else arrived—and we know that because there were no other tire tracks beside the BMW's."

"What do you suppose he was waiting for while he was sitting there?"

"My guess would be that he was waiting on dawn's first light. He was waiting for the sun to rise so that he could see what he was doing more clearly and thereby increase his enjoyment at Kathy's expense."

Charlie checked the preliminary work sheet that he was handed when he first arrived. "The coroner put the male victim's time of death at about two o'clock in the morning, and he put Kathy's about three hours later, somewhere about five AM." Charlie looked at his watch. It was eleven-fifteen in the morning on a bright sunny day. "If dawn was about five fifteen, then he tortured her for about an hour before he killed her."

"You are pretty much accurate with your timeline, Charlie, but I have a few more things to add, and they make everything a bit more bizarre. Take a closer look at the foot of the tree. Notice that the ground has been well stamped on, and many of the surrounding leaves have been broken into small pieces. We found thousands of small drops of blood that speckled the ground to the left and right of the tree, but the base itself had absolutely no blood there."

Thoughts were whirling around inside Charlie's head as he slowly said, "Can we assume, Detective, that it is a given that she lost a great deal of blood while she was being tortured?"

"Yes, lots of blood."

"Can we also assume that in order to catch the blood as she was bleeding out, that he had spread a tarp of some sort on the ground, probably under her feet, and that would catch most of the blood and other items that he might have overlooked."

"Very clever, Detective Glass. You are referring to other items such as semen."

"Yes, semen." Charlie continued, "Let's assume that he raped her and then pulled out because he did not want to leave traceable semen behind."

Detective Wahl hesitated a moment and then said, "Maybe you are right but I don't think so. We know he shoved something in her orifices, but we don't think it was his dick, because that's not the way this kind of guy gets off. Experience with these types of cases tells us that he likes to watch the pain and degradation that he is causing while he jerks off."

Charlie disagreed with the dectective, but since it was the more experienced Wahl who stated this opinion, Charlie accepted it for the moment.

Charlie gathered up his courage, reviewed the funny feeling he was getting so far from their discussion, and decided to ask the million-dollar question of his fellow detective. Charlie threw out the question. "I guess that you have seen this type of thing before, haven't you, Detective Wahl?" He watched Detective Wahl's facial expressions very carefully, but there was nothing to read on his face, one way or the other. This man was a highly trained professional and had full and absolute control of himself at all times.

"Yes, Charlie.. I have seen this very same type of thing once before. I find it very interesting that you ask me this specific question at this particular moment."

"When was this—and kindly give me some details!"

"I can remember it like it was yesterday. You know how certain things, some good and some bad, stay with you and play games with your mind. It was eighteen years ago, and I know that for a fact because that was when I was transferred to this unit. That murder was the seventh case that I worked on that year, and seven, which is supposed to be a lucky number, never worked for me. Tonight, I was watching your reactions to my walking you around from spot to spot without missing anything. You had to be thinking, how can Joe Wahl know about this and that in such a short space of time?

"Charlie, I know what you are thinking. You are saying to yourself, what if good old Joe Wahl is the killer. Maybe that is why he knows what happened out here without really trying. How could Joe Wahl know all these things without being himself involved?"

"These are good questions, Charlie but the answer is even better. I know exactly what happened here because I saw it all, every single detail, every drop of blood, everything and anything connected with this case, because I have lived it for the past eighteen years, and it has never been far away from my thoughts.

"You see, Charlie, I knew just where to look and what to look for because the killer, eighteen years ago chained his victim to the same tree. He also went right to that spot and had his smokes, but eighteen years ago, that ballsy son of a bitch brought himself a lawn chair. I found the indentations in the ground where he had sat."

"And how about that earlier victim, was it the same type of torture?"

"Yes, Charlie; she suffered through the exact same kind of hell, and I couldn't solve the case then. I'm hoping that you will let me be your number two backup on this one. I know more about this case then the killer himself! I did not solve that case. It is the only unsolved homicide case on my record, and I will beg you if I have to. Charlie, let me work with you. Nobody knows it better. Nobody will work harder then I will. Give it some thought and let me know. I will owe you big time if you let me assist."

"I promise you, Joe, that we can talk about this. Right now I have a few more questions that I need answered. Obviously, this case is unsolved, and therefore the files will be available in the open-ended case books. You could save me a lot of reading and discovery time, so more than likely you will be my number two."

"But, Joe, I have to warn you. Right now I think you are the prime suspect, and you look good for the murder. So if we are working together, you'll be looking at the case, and I will be looking at the case—and I will be looking at you."

CHAPTER FOURTEEN

"ONE WEEK LATER"

Charlie turned quickly and looked behind him. He had just heard someone call out his name.

She stood a dozen paces from him, a tall, slender girl with dark eyes and close-cropped brown hair. She wore a fencing jacket and held a rapier/sword in her right hand. In her left she held a protective fencing mask. She was looking directly at Charlie and laughing at the same time.

Her teeth were white and even and possibly a trifle long, and a band of freckles crossed her small nose and the upper portions of her well-tanned cheeks. There was that special air of vitality about her, which is attractive in many ways quite different from just mere comeliness. This was especially true when viewed from Charlie's vantage point of having known so many women.

She saluted him with her blade. "En garde, Charlie!" she said.

§

My name, of course, is Charles Glass, and I do answer to being called Charlie, but at that particular moment in time, I was tired and was not in the best of moods for any games.

I had just come off of a full two-hour session of fencing with my fencing instructor on the mats, where we were going at it hot and heavy against each other. Today was my final session with him, and after twelve long months of training and conditioning, I had finally advanced to the level of where I could take him to a draw. This was a real accomplishment, and I was very proud of my having accomplished so much in such a little amount of time.

Ever since I was a kid, I was completely enchanted by the use of a sword! My first hero in life was John Carter, my fellow Earthman who was transported to the planet Mars in the science-fiction story written by Edgar Rice Burroughs.

As soon as I was able to afford it, I began taking instructions in how to fence, and surprisingly, I was pretty good at it. In my imagination, I was John Carter fighting the bad guys and defending the pretty ladies. I kept at it all through my teens and into my early adult years until now, I had become quite an accomplished fencer, able to hold my own with anyone and everyone.

This was my personal form of escape from the murder-and-mayhem police cases that I would be asked to solve in my job as a Los Angeles Sheriff's Department Homicide Detective. Fencing was my way of escaping from the reality of blood and gore that I was forced to see upon an almost-daily basis as part of my job. Today was one of my rare days off from the job, and as always when I had the time, I had engaged my friend and fencing instructor into a match that would tire me out to the deepest part of my soul and allow me not to think about death and killers for a-while.

After years and years of practice and learning the ins and outs of fencing, I finally was able to move up to my friend's skill level, and could duel with him evenly, of which I was very proud. My friend and instructor was the equivalent of a black belt in the very fine art of fencing, and for me to duel with him and come out even gave me the same top rating he had. I was so very pleased that now, as a "black belt," I was at the top of the ladder where my being a product of the highly aggressive and competitive 1980s had taken me. I had fought the good fight and won. I was a happy guy.

Just a few minutes earlier, I had received hugs and well-wishes from all of my fencing friends at the studio when I had said my final farewells to them. I had walked outside and gone over to the nearby baseball field, where I was just standing there quietly, drinking a soft drink, when the girl with the mask and fencing equipment suddenly had appeared.

"Who the hell are you?" I asked as I noticed another fencing jacket, a mask and a sword lying at her feet. Obviously she had something in mind.

"No questions and no answers," she said. "At least not until we've fenced. I want to see for myself, if you are as good as everyone says you are. You're not afraid of a mere girl, are you?"

I walked over and picked up the equipment. I could see that it would be easier to fence rather than argue with her. The fact that she knew my name disturbed me, and the more that I thought about it, the more the girl seemed somehow familiar.

It seemed best to humor her, I decided, as I shrugged into the jacket and buckled it on. I picked up the blade, tested it with a few simple moves. Satisfied, I then pulled on the mask.

"All right," I said, sketching out a brief fencing salute to her, and then I advanced slowly toward her.

She moved forward also, and we met somewhere near first base on the flat baseball field.

I didn't bother to tell her that I was nearly exhausted from my dueling with my instructor for the past few hours. I considered this to be an extra endurance training session.

She came at me very fast with a bare-feint-feint thrust!

My riposte was nearly twice as fast as her first move, but she was really good and was able to parry it, and came back at me with equal speed.

This was proving to be an excellent match, and I began to enjoy myself. I began a slow backward retreat, trying to draw her out and expose a weakness, but she showed me nothing and laughed at me for a moment before she attacked again, which pushed me a few steps backward, as she was pressing me hard.

She was impressively well trained, and very athletic in all her quick responses. She obviously knew how good she was, and she wanted to show off what she could do, and I knew that I had to be ready for anything she would throw at me.

I was familiar with most of her classic attacks, but it was when she would improvise something new that gave me the most problems. She almost got through my defenses twice, in a low line attack, and I chalked up that move to something that I had never seen before but would be ready for it if I ever saw it again. She was teaching me things by actual combat that my friend and instructor never gave me. I was most impressed with my opponent at that moment even though I made sure that I did not show it.

I caught her with a beautifully executed double-stop-thrust as soon as she slowed down her offensive moves. She had to fall back sharply, and I heard her curse softly, but good-naturedly, as she acknowledged my excellent counter-move. I was really proud of the way my body responded automatically to the ebb and flow of our engagement. I felt that I really was at the top of my game, and I was suddenly loving this duel being fought on a baseball field in the middle of the west side of Los Angeles.

I do not ordinarily like to fence with women, no matter how good they are, but this time I discovered that I was completely enjoying myself. The skill and grace with which she carried the attacks and bore them at me, gave me pleasure to behold and respond too.

I found myself thinking about what kind of mind did she have behind that mask? At first, I had just wanted to tire her out quickly in order to conclude the match and put some questions to her. Now that we were really getting into it, I found myself wanting to prolong this highly enjoyable encounter. I was pleased that she did not tire readily.

I lost track of time as we stamped back and forth along the baseball path with our blades clicking steadily. A long while must have passed, though, before she finally stamped her heel to the ground as a signal, and then threw up her blade in a final salute to me.

She tore off her mask and gave me a great big smile. "Thank you," she said breathing heavily.

I returned her salute and drew off my own mask. I turned and fumbled with the jacket buckles, and before I realized it, she had approached and kissed me softly on the cheek.

I felt momentarily confused but I managed to smile at her.

Before I could say anything, she took my arm and turned me back in the direction from which we had just come. "You are wonderful," she said. "I think that you deserve a reward. What do you say to a quickie at my place? It isn't far."

CHAPTER FIFTEEN

Her name was Barbara Bennett, and she had been a United States fencing team member for several years. She would do workouts at the same place where I was always upgrading my skills with my sword fighting.

Now I was remembering why she had looked so familiar to me. Whenever my instructor and I would do one of our special weapons workouts, a small group of students and teachers would gather around us to watch. I remembered her now as the tall, rather cute one, who had that great-looking body, and who was always looking at me from a distance. Well, she was no longer any distance away now!

We had walked over to a main street in Westwood called Veteran Avenue, which was about three long blocks away from the baseball field. When we finally arrived at her place, we walked up the two flights of stairs that led to her neatly furnished apartment.

We had casually talked as we walked, and I found out that she was an assistant manager at a local McDonalds restaurant, where she worked four days a week. Today was one of her days off, and she had gone to the dueling academy for a workout, where she saw the final match that I had with my instructor. The rest is history in that here I was in her apartment, waiting for her to come out of the bathroom to where she had excused herself, and went to wash up.

Her only instructions to me were to please close the curtains, and to leave some lights on in the bedroom. She also added, as she closed the bathroom door behind her, "Would you please pull back the covers on the bed, and kindly strip down to your shorts."

This rather surprised me in that I had never met any female as aggressive as Barbara was. She seemed to really like to be in charge, and with my being a guest in her home, I was okay with that.

I did all the household chores that she had asked of me, and I did strip down as I sat on the bed, waiting for her to make her appearance. I was curious as to what I would be seeing when she came out of the bathroom. Would I be seeing a naked Barbara, or a sexy-outfitted lady, or perhaps even something else?

As it turned out, it was to be the something else, and I was pleasantly surprised by this girl who definitely enjoyed being different.

§

Barbara had stepped into the bathroom and washed up. She shed all her clothing and looked at her naked figure in the full-length bathroom mirror.

She liked what she saw and went about getting dressed in that new kinky outfit that looked like fun when she picked it out at that sexy lingerie boutique in Westwood.

She stepped into what seemed to be the leg portion of a black thong, and slid it up over her hips. She stared down at it, trying to figure out how to put on the top, and finally realized that the bra portion consisted of several straps that surrounded her breasts in a triangle shape with little chains draping over each breast. She pulled it on, exhilarated by the feel of the cold silver chains brushing against her nipples.

There were five chains over each breast, and … oh… each center chain had a separated metal ring in the middle and that one sat right over her nipple. As she adjusted the leather straps on the bra so that they sat just right, her nipples blossomed, sticking forward through the rings.

She then opened the shoe box to find a special pair of black leather shoes, with four-inch spike heels, and very wide ankle straps with silver studs. She pulled the shoes on and fastened all the straps.

She forced herself to peek in the full length mirror. Her eyes widened. She looked … erotic … wicked … and wildly sexy.

She noted that a chain draped itself over the crotch of her new leather outfit. She flicked at it with her finger, and realized that there was a slit in the fabric beneath it, running the entire length of the crotch. It was this opening that she hoped would allow Charlie to find her special area, and she was hoping that he would know all kinds of ways to make use of it. A final touch of perfume sprayed here and there, and then she was ready to open the door.

Charlie jumped to his feet with his gaze completely riveted upon her.

Barbara was just loving the look on his face as she walked over to Charlie and kissed him on the lips with a light feather touch. Then she pushed him a few feet backwards until he was sitting up on the edge of the bed watching her with very curious eyes.

Knowing that he was completely focused on her butt, she slowly turned and walked away from him and went over to the music corner, where she pressed the correct buttons and her favorite slow-sounding rhythm filled the room.

In her younger days, Barbara had worked in a local high-end bar, where she was one of the featured pole dancers. She had worked out a very sexy series of moves that she began to perform in front of Charlie, who was just sitting there, perfectly still, with his mouth hanging open in complete surpnse. Obviously, he did not know what to expect from her.

When she had mentioned the word 'quickie' to him after their duel, he probably expected to jump into her bed, do his thing, and then get out in no time at all. That was not the way she liked to do things.

Only when she was fencing did she do things quickly and precisely. When it came to sex, the slower and more original it could be, the better it always was.

There she was, swaying back and forth in front of him, when suddenly he could not sit still any more. He had to touch her, caress her and make passionate love to her. He stood up and put his arms around her, and held her closely, as he gently put his lips on hers in an extremely soft and very sensual kiss.

Her response was also surprisingly gentle, and she slowly forced her tongue between his lips where it met absolutely no resistance.

They clung to each other for a few minutes until his hands began to roam down her back. The music in the background simply faded away as he gently grabbed her buttocks and pulled her tightly against him.

She pulled her lips away from his so that she could catch her breath. She did like the feel of his hands on her butt, and she snuggled up tighter against his tall and hard body.

Still standing, he suddenly spun her completely around until she was standing directly in front of him. She could feel the hardness of his erection pressed up against her. She noted that somehow or other, he had lost the pair of shorts that he had been wearing a few minutes ago, and this excited her more.

A sudden jolt of electricity flashed through her body as both of his hands went around her, and his hands moved up to her breasts where he began a gentle rubbing against her nipples that were still protruding at full attention through the circular openings in the black bra that she was still wearing. One of his hands slid down and moved about on her flat belly, and it was simply wonderful having her stomach rubbed at the very same time as one of her nipples was being pulled.

In a very practiced move, he grabbed hold of the top leather bra with all the little silver chains rattling about, and flipped it over her head. She was still standing in front of him facing away, as both his hands freely moved all over her free-standing breasts.

As she was enjoying the playtime that Charles was having with her boobs, a random thought came to her. *Can a guy tell by his sense of touch, if a girl has had a boob job?* Can Charlie tell what used to be an athletic, flat-chested girl was now a very well-endowed B-cup bra-size female?

When she had the surgery a few years ago, she thought about making her breasts even bigger, but decided not to do so for two very good reasons. The first one was that, as the famous old saying goes, "more than a handful is wasted," and secondly, they would get in the way whenever she was playing at being a sword fighter.

What pleased her, after spending many sleepless nights thinking about it, was that she seemed to not have lost any of the sensations that touching her breasts gave her after the gel implants were put in. It was hard to tell, but maybe the sensation was even greater now, because after her surgery she felt much more sexy than she ever did before. She greatly enjoyed watching the guys who never gave her a look before suddenly paying attention to her every move. A man's weakness is definitely a woman's tits. *Screw them,* she would think. *I'm in command now.* With her slim and athletic body, and a set of good-sized knockers, she had her pick of the male population for miles around.

And her pick for today was the famous Charles Glass. She had watched him this afternoon and saw that he was extremely good with a pointed blade in his hand. The question that she wanted to find out now, was if he was any good with his "personal blade."

CHAPTER SIXTEEN

Pure, raw lust tore through Detective Second Grade Charlie Glass on his day off. He was thinking that this was probably the best use of his time that he had ever done before. All thoughts of the job were completely gone from his mind as he pursued his own personal bodily needs with this amazingly exciting and wonderful female.

Turning his concentration back to his newly discovered wild woman, he knew that she was enjoying wearing those black leather shorts and those high-heeled shoes, but they had to go. They were just in his way. With very little effort at all, he guided her into the removal of the shorts and shoes, and she stood before him now, as naked as he was, and that was another good thing.

Barbara herself was swamped with many different sensations as she assisted Charlie in the removal of her shorts and shoes. She thought that the sexy clothing was a wonderful idea, and they were fun for a few minutes, but obviously Charlie did not want them on her, and so she abandoned them without a second thought. She had absolutely no problem shedding them as she once again put her arms around his neck and pressed herself up against him. His lean and rock-hard body felt good to her.

He was holding her against him effortlessly with her feet off the ground, and she was just dangling there as he held her with his strong masculine arms. She felt his heavy erection pressing against her thighs, and this was greatly exciting to her! He was BIG and she knew that she was going to love every moment of the wonderful sex with him that was only moments away.

Charlie stared down at her, seeing that her pale blue eyes were sparkling with a hunger, a need that only he could satisfy right now. *Wow,* he thought. *This is one really hot woman!*

He had encountered this particular kind of female before, and he knew that it would take a lot of different climaxes and positions before she would be satisfied. Charlie was quite confident that he knew just what had to be done, and he felt that he had the proper training for the job.

Outside of his police files and all the good and bad things that he read in them, being able to pleasure a woman was always one of his main goals in life. He had put in a lot of field work learning just what went where and why, and he felt that he was at the top of the leader board when it came to women. He realized that he did not understand the female mind, and he had no clue as to how to decipher their emotions, but when it came to their fooling around with sex, he was definitely the right guy.

Enough with the thinking and more with the doing. This little lady was red-hot and more than ready to go. He held her close and spun them both around in a circle just to celebrate their nakedness, and the fun that was in store for the two of them. He loved the way her hands clenched his shoulders, and her nails as they lightly dug into his flesh. He set her down gently on her back on top of the soft and giving bed, and then leaned over her while her fingers speared into his curly hair as she pulled him down toward her waiting mouth.

She was loving it. She loved his lips on her lips, so hungry and deep as they continued to exchange more passionate kisses that sent flames rushing through all of her pulsating parts.

He gently moved himself between her moving thighs, and found no resistance at all from her. She seemed hot and ready. He heard her whisper softly into his ear, "Make me feel you, Charlie. Give me everything you've got. I can handle it.

Without another word, Charlie entered her place of pleasure and penetrated it very slowly, going back and forth and in and out. He would go a little bit farther with each push until he was finally in as far as he could go. Her sounds of pleasure began to multiply as he slowly increased the pace and he pounded away at her very yielding body.

Charlie, who always prided himself at being a breast msn, had hold of one of her boobs while he was servicing her. In life, at least in his young life so far, there was nothing like entering a woman, pounding away at her, and at the same time playing with her boobs. Sometimes, he thought, life was good, and this was one of those special moments.

After a few more minutes of these delightful sensations, Charlie took full advantage of his being very strong and Barbara being so slender and light weight. While he was still inside her, he held her tightly and rolled himself onto his back, which put her on top of him in an upright sitting position. She was actually sitting on his lap, and now she could control their movements as she went up and down on him with a great smile on her pretty face.

It was quite obvious to him that she had been on top of guys before, because she went at it with a wild recklessness and it was only moments later when she rocked for the final time and moved herself backward, which caused him to completely slip out of her vagina. The two of them collapsed and neither of them moved for several long and wonderful minutes.

He would have been content to just lie there and relive the moment, but not so Barbara. She began to fondle and kiss his shrunken penis, and under her extremely well educated hands, he began to grow hard once again. She was a miracle worker!

Charlie was thinking that this was the most sexual woman that he had ever gone to bed with, and if he happened to survive this experience with her, he planned on courting her in a proper way and try and make some sort of an arrangement with her, if he lived. Not only was she cute with a great personality and body, but she was way beyond great in bed. Someone like Barbara was absolutely quite rare, and he knew that it was in his best interest to keep her in his life. He was no fool.

Charlie knew that he was running out of energy and that his "gas tank" was almost empty, but he would try for one more exceptional experience. He wanted to give her something special to remember him by.

Without speaking a word to her, he again lifted her up and put her face-down on the bed. He put enough pressure on her shoulders so that she had to lean down on her arms in order to keep her balance. He put his arms around her waist and pulled her rear end up until she was on her knees.

He then slipped himself carefully between her legs, being so very delicate to not hurt her since she was probably very sore and tender from all the friction the area was getting from him. Since she was so moist from all the other fooling around that they had been doing, he was able to slip his full length inside her quite easily.

Now, in this position, the woman is actually quite helpless. All she can do is to use her hands to help her keep her balance while she in being held down on the mattress. It is the man who is in full control, and Charlie took full advantage of the situation by pounding away as hard and as long as he could. Unfortunately, he was able to only last a minute or so, but from the noises coming from Barbara, beneath him, he knew that she was enjoying his male dominance over her.

Moments later, they both collapsed into each other's arms, pulled the covers over themselves and promptly fell into a deep and highly satisfied sleep.

CHAPTER SEVENTEEN

Charlie arrived an hour and a half early at the Sheriff's Station Headquarters on that Monday morning. He needed to get his thoughts back into focus on the case that was being labeled as SDD-HC14. This stood for Sheriff's Detective Division Homicide Case Number Fourteen.

As he flipped through the few pages that so far made up the Homicide case book, he realized that there was nothing of any great interest or concern in the file. It was very "plain vanilla." It was definitely time for his own personal report upon his observations and thoughts to be added to the book so that all the fact and ideas would be made available for anyone else to see and be brought up to date.

He dated his entry as 6/6/86 and recorded his name, rank and serial number next to it. He read and re-read the specific details of the murder scene, and wrote in the margin, that as per his understanding of the case so far, everything was entered entirely accurate. He also thought that Detective Joe Wahl's scribbled handwritten notes left nothing out and were extremely detailed.

Charlie was still bothered by the fact that Detective Joe Wahl had so much accurate information about the case long before the murder-lab techs had made their up-to-the-minute reports. Joe seemed to know the details, item for item, before the lab released their findings. What was most bothersome was that Joe Wahl was not off-point on anything. Not on anything. That did not seem to be humanly possible unless he had insider or first-hand information.

Charlie decided to move on and come back to Detective Wahl's possible connection to the crime at a later date. He kept asking himself why Joe, who had seen an almost perfect duplication of the crime at the exact same location as he said he saw eighteen years ago, did not say anything. He only spoke up after Charlie asked him about it. Not only was this very strange, but it was downright suspicious, and that made Detective Joe Wahl a suspect in Charlie's mind.

Eighteen years is an extremely long time for someone to remember so many details, and yet Joe did. Not only did he remember the exact description of the events that took place, he told his story as if he was actually there.

The question Charlie kept asking himself over and over was why did Wahl hold back from telling about his first-hand information. There was only two possible answers to that question. Either Joe was the guilty party or else he thought that giving up such detailed information would make him look like he was the guilty party.

Charlie's mind was going round and round in circles, and he decided to move on with his entry and the tape recording of the murder book. Charlie noted that he had sent out an APB to every jurisdiction asking if they had any unsolved murder cases going back eighteen years that would fit his case. He gave them a brief set of details and hoped to get a response from someone. A serial killer who duplicated his techniques would not wait so many years between his crimes. Somewhere and someplace could possibly provide an answer.

Charlie moved on. He next began to enter the information on the male victim of the Mulholland Crime Scene. This was a simple and uncomplicated entry that only took a few minutes to do.

The male victim's name was Palmer Peterson, and he worked as a stunt man for one of the local Hollywood studios. There was nothing in his history beyond saying that he had several unpaid parking tickets, and that he was single and was twenty nine years of age.

His cause of death was reported as a single bullet to the head as noted in the detailed lab report. There were traces of paper and glass found with the bullet, and the glass matched the window glass from the BMW's driver's side through which the single bullet was fired. The paper was from a plain brown paper bag, available at any shopping market in the area, and was given no further consideration, as was the glass from the window of the BMW.

The bullet had entered the male victim's head 1.5 centimeters forward of the right ear which indicated that he was on his knees and looking down at the female when the bullet entered his skull, thereby killing him instantly. He bled out quickly and any and all blood and body fluids matched his DNA, leading to the conclusion that the female who fled the car moments later was not struck by the one and only shot fired into the car.

The bullet was recovered intact. His next of kin were notified, and the body had not as of yet been claimed.

§

Charlie added his hand-printed comment in the column next to where the report said the bullet was recovered intact. This was called a flag and it called attention to the comment being made.

Charlie wrote and then attached the paper to the file as follows:

> It has to be noted here that, acting as lead investigator on this double homicide death, I, on site, specifically asked detective Joe Wahl many questions, the answers of which were unknown to myself or any other investigators on the scene at that time.

The ease and accuracy of Detective Wahl's answers made him a suspect in my mind and I wrote out in greater detail my thoughts on the matter of Joe Wahl and this double homicide, as well as the homicide that took place at the exact location on Mulholland Drive some eighteen years ago.

My letter to this effect and the facts as I presently understand them were given to my assigning Sheriff's Captain, who put them under seal until this case moves further along.

I am planning on using Detective Wahl as my number two back-up detective so that I can keep an eye on him, and so that I can pull other information from him that might be of great importance to the case.

I have been told that a full-time team of detectives have been assigned undercover to watch his movements, and to this date even I, knowing that they are watching, can't figure out who they are.

My compliments to the observers.

Respectfully submitted
Charles Glass, Sheriff's Investigator.

CHAPTER EIGHTEEN
SHERIFF'S DETECTIVE DIVISION HOMICIDE CASE #14

§

SPECIAL ENTRY BEING MADE INTO EVIDENCE BY SHERIFF'S INVESTIGATOR SERGEANT CHARLES GLASS.

§

The person of interest in this exceptional case is that of the deceased Kathy Barnes.

Kathy Barnes was the daughter of the all-powerful Speaker of the Los Angeles County Department of Ways and Means Committee, John Ganz. Initial investigation of Speaker John Ganz has turned up several disturbing items, which I do not wish to disclose at this moment in my required report.

I only wish to comment that my informal conversations with the previously named Speaker caused me to go a bit deeper into the background of Mr. Ganz and have led me to the possiblity that the murder of his daughter Kathy might be connected to a business conflict that has not come to light yet with a building contractor out of Chicago who was having trouble getting permits to build his projected high-rise project in downtown Los Angeles.

It has not been established if threats were made, but my investigation into the background of the Chicago contractor has taken me to the door of a possible connection to organized crime. Just what organized crime, our own city Ways and Means chairman, and the death of one Kathy Barnes have to do with each other is presently beyond my knowledge.

It must be noted here for the record that the concern I previously stated that my number-two back-up detective on the double homicide that is in ongoing investigation has been of the greatest help and value to this case, and at present I am highly doubtful of my earlier belief that Detective Joe Wahl is somehow connected to the case(s).

It has now been sixteen days into the investigation of the double homicide, and the details of the deaths and behind-the-scenes goings-on are becoming much clearer.

Further secure notes to follow.

Charles Glass—Lead Investigator, Sheriff's Department

CHAPTER NINETEEN

COMMUNICATION TO DETECTIVE SERGEANT CHARLES GLASS—SHERIFF'S DEPARTMENT, CITY OF LOS ANGELES, CALIFORNIA

§

FOR THE EYES ONLY OF DETECTIVE CHARLES GLASS

Hello, Detective Glass:

This response to your recent letter asking for any known connection between the City of Los Angeles and organized crime follows.

We are unable to draw any conclusions based upon the few bits of factual information that you have presented to us.

However, we are able to state that we agree with your suggestion that there very well could be a direct connection to the City of Los Angeles's building contracts, which come out of your city hall address, and the background and underground activities of organized crime.

We would need much more specific information from your end in order to tie together some of the answers that you are requesting re any connection with the double homicide you are currently investigating.

As follows please find the background information you requested.

If I can be of further assistance, please contact me at the same written address as per your original inquiry.

Most sincerely yours,
Sharlene Sachs—Historical Crime Files

§

Benjamin "Bugsy" Siegel
Born Feb. 28, 1906
Williamsbury, New York, USA
Died June 20, 1947 at age 41
Cause of death: homicide
Resting place: Hollywood Forever Cemetery
Resident: L.A., Calif.
Other known names:
Benny, Bug, Bugs, Bugsy
Ethnicity: Jewish
Occupation(s):
Gangster and casino owner

§

Bugsy Siegel was a Jewish American mobster who was known as one of the most "infamous and feared gangsters of his day." He was described as handsome and charismatic, and he became one of the first front-page-celebrity gangsters in the

United States of America. He was also a driving force behind the development of casinos and gambling on the Las Vegas, Nevada, Strip.

Siegel was not only influential with the Jewish Mob but, like his friend and fellow gangster Meyer Lansky, he also held significant influence with the Italian-Jewish national crime syndicate.

Siegel was one of the founders and leaders of Murder, Inc. and became a leading bootlegger during prohibition. After prohibition was repealed in 1933, he turned to gambling. In 1936, he left New York and moved to Los Angeles, California.

His time as a mobster (although he eventually ran his own operation) was mainly as a hit man and he was noted as having great skill with guns and violence.

In his middle twenties, Siegel befriended Meyer Lansky, who was forming a small Mob whose activities were gambling and car theft. Meyer Lansky, who had a run-in with famous mobster Lucky Luciano, saw a need for the Jewish boys from his New York neighborhood to organize in the same manner as the Italians and Irish. The first person Meyer Lansky recruited was Bugsy Siegel.

Siegel became a bootlegger and was involved with several eastern and west coast cities. He began making friends in the Los Angeles area, where his major interests seemed to lie. He was thinking ahead with Los Angeles in mind.

A famous article was printed in the *New York Times* and made a big hit on the west coast where he was beginning to make a name for himself as a "made" man.

The article read, and we quote it here:

"Bugsy Siegel never hesitated when danger threatened himself or his friends. While others tried to figure out what was the best move, Bugsy was already out in the field shooting."

When it came to action, there was no one better than the "bug"man.

§

Bugsy was also a friend of Al Capone out of Chicago. When there was a warrant out for Capone's arrest on a murder charge, Siegel allowed him to hide out with an aunt until everything calmed down. In return for the favor, Capone and the Chicago boys lent their support to Bugsy in all of his ventures.

It was in Hollywood that Bugsy had the most success. He had Mob backers now in Chicago and New York, and he used their support in getting things done his way.

In Hollywood, Bugsy was welcomed into the highest circles, and he was befriended by many movie stars. He became a known associate with George Raft, Clark Gable, Gary Cooper, and Cary Grant. A few studio executives also claimed his friendship. He was most friendly with studio heads Louis B. Meyer and Jack L. Warner. Jean Harlow was a personal/close friend, and he made her godmother to his daughter Millicent Siegel.

Bugsy Siegel led an exceptional life in Hollywood as he bought and personally sold large tracts of land in Los Angeles County, and this is where he first became connected with members of the Los Angeles city council—it is our opinion that your investigation should start with the relationship of Siegel and members of the city council up to and including the years just after his death.

Alleged paperwork, which I have not seen, is thought to express agreements with Bugsy's successors in the crime syndicate from his lifetime into the present era.

A direct tie-in is the possible punishment-death of a city council member's daughter in the double homicide you are investigating.

Coming back to the last year of Bugsy Siegel's life, we find that he would throw lavish parties at his Beverly Hills home, and parts of the guest lists we have been able to secure have shown us the names of members of the Los Angeles city council in attendance.

While their being at his home proves nothing, a question has to be cleared up if the Mob still holds influence over the members who followed these party friends of Siegel.

And finally, we note that he had personal relationships with Tony Curtis, Phil Silvers, and Frank Sinatra and his "rat pack" friends, who would be his guests in Las Vegas at some of the hotels he had interests in.

The earlier murder eighteen years ago, in our opinion, was not a serial killer. We believe that it was one of the enforcers for the Mob there in Los Angeles, and that killer just repeated his techniques since they were successful and were not caught at that time.

This is the reason that no other murders that

have occurred within this time frame have shown up in any of the crime records.

Kindly make up your own mind on this but we are closing down our search which we had done at your request for similar signs that would have been left by a serial killer within the confines of the United States.

And one final note of interest to me and perhaps to you personally, having nothing to do with your pending investigation follows:

To show the strong ties that the Mob had from the 1930s through the present 1980s, please note the following Hollywood/Los Angeles books, movies and articles celebrating their achievements.

1) Bugsy Siegel was the basis for the Moe Green character in Mario Puzo's novel and subsequent movie *The Godfather*.

2) Sergio Leone's film *Once upon a Time in America* is loosely based on the lives of Bugsy Siegel and Meyer Lansky.

3) *Bugsy: The Novel* is a semi-fictional biography of Bugsy Siegel by a noted Hollywood writer.

4) Bugsy Siegel is a minor character in the famous movie *The Black Dahlia*.

5) The Bugsy Siegel character has appeared in television and broadway stage productions for years and years.

He is a leading character in Jonathan Stewart's television series The Making of the Mob.

CHAPTER TWENTY

Detectives Glass and Wahl were talking quietly over coffee at one of the local Starbucks coffee shops in Hollywood that was not very far away from the Hollywood Forever Cemetery where Bugsy Siegel had been buried.

Joe Wahl had told Charlie that he was most impressed with Bugsy Siegel, who dabbled as a part-time screenplay writer for one of the studios that he had a connection with.

Joe had gone through their files on Bugsy from 1947 and had made a copy of a movie that Bugsy was pushing to get made.

It was only a very short story and Charlie agreed to listen to Joe reading it to him so that he could get a feel for just who and what Bugsy Siegel was in his Hollywood days.

Joe began to read in a soft voice that did not carry beyond Charlie Glass, who was sitting beside him.

TRUELOVE

A POTENTIAL SCREENPLAY BY BUGSY SIEGEL – 1/2/47

§

"My name is Joe! That is what my creator, Milton Davidson, calls me. He is a computer programmer, and I am his program! He created me originally, but of course, I have grown and developed in all sorts of ways since then, and I am quite an impressive program now!

I live in a separate section of the government's computer complex. I live in section SW-452, but I can't tell you exactly where because it is a secret. I know all of the special secrets from around the entire world. I know everything—well, almost everything!

I am Milton's private program. I am his Joe and I am not *just* a program to him. The computer section that I live in is his private section. He does not let anyone else use it. He understands more about computers than anyone in the world, and I— and the computer I live in—are his experimental models.

He has made me speak through my computer better than any other computer can. It's just a matter of matching sounds to symbols, he told me. He said that is the way it also works in the human brain even though we do not know what symbols there are in the brain.

Milton has never married, thought he is nearly forty years old. He has never found the right woman, he told me.

One day he said to me, "I'll find her yet, Joe. I'm going to find the best woman in the world! I am going to have true love, and you are going to help me find her, Joe! Lately, all you and I are doing is fixing the problems of the world. I want us to solve my problem. I want you to find me true love."

I said to Milton, "What is true love?"

"Never mind that! True love is just an abstract thing. I just want you to find me the ideal girl. You are connected to all of the computers in the world-complex. That will allow you to reach the data base of every human being in the world.

"What I want you to do is to eliminate them all by groups and classes until we are left with only one person. That person will be the perfect woman for me."

I said, "I am ready."

He said, "Eliminate all men first." It was easy.

His words activated symbols in my computing valves. I could reach out to make contact with the accumulated data on every human being in the world. At his spoken word, I withdrew from 3,484,982,872 men. I kept contact with 4,788,456,201 women.

He said, "Eliminate all women younger that twenty-five and all older than forty. Then eliminate all with an IQ under 120 and all with a height above five foot three inches." He then gave me exact body measurements, and then he eliminated women with living children, and then those women with various genetic characteristics. His final instuctions were, and I quote him here, "No women with blond hair. I don't like blondes."

After two weeks, we were down to 235 women! They all spoke English very well. Milton clearly stated that he did not want a language problem.

"I can't interview 235 women," he said. "It would take too much time and people would discover what I am doing."

I knew that Milton could get in trouble with all of this because he was having me do things that I was not designed to do. No one knew about what we were doing and we planned to keep it that way.

"It's none of their business," he said, and the skin on his face would grow red.

Milton brought in pictures of women. "Those are pictures of three beauty contest winners," he said. "Do any of the 235 match?"

Eight were very good matches, and Milton said, "It's good that you have their information in your data banks. I want you to study all the requirements and needs in the job market here at our company, and then make arrangements to have them assigned to work here. Only one at a time, of course." He stood very still and seemed to be thinking to himself. Then he added, "Also have them hired in alphabetical order."

This is one of the things I am not designed to do. Shifting people from job to job for personal reasons is called manipulation! I could do it now because Milton had arranged it. I was not supposed to do it for anyone but him, and we never talked much about this.

The first girl arrived a week later. Milton's face turned red when he saw her. He spoke as though it were suddenly hard for him to speak. They were together a great deal, and Milton started to ignore me and gave me none of his attention.

I heard him say, a few days later, that he would like to take her to dinner. He suggested a nearby Italian restaurant that he had heard good things about.

The next day he came to me and said in a sad-sounding voice that his date was not so good. Somehow, there was something missing between himself and the girl.

He said, "I want you to understand, Joe. She is a beautiful girl and all of that, and she met all of my physical descriptions of what she should look like. But I did not feel anything special towards her. I did not feel that she was my true love. Let us go on to the next one."

It was the same thing with all eight of the ladies! They were very much alike. They smiled a great deal and had pleasant voices and all that, but Milton always found them to be not right.

He said to me, "I can't understand it, Joe. You and I have picked out the eight women who in all the world look and sound the best to me. They are all ideal! But why don't any of them please me?"

I said, "Do you please them?"

His eyebrows moved and he pushed one fist hard against his other hand. "That's it, Joe. I never realized that true love has to be a two-way-street. If I am not their ideal man, then they won't act in such a way as to be my ideal woman. I must make myself into their true love, too. But how do I do that?"

I noticed that he seemed to be thinking about that problem for the rest of the day.

The next morning he came to me and said, "I'm going to leave it up to you, Joe. All up to you. You have my data bank in your computer system, and I am going to tell you everyting I know about myself, and you can make an entry about me on your memory file."

"What will I do with the data-bank memory file once I have it all put together, Milton?"

"Then you could match my information to that

82

list of the original 237 females."

"I want you to arrange to have each of the women undergo a psychiatric examination. Enter the results into their data banks and compare them with mine. The results should solve all of my problems."

For weeks, Milton talked to me. He told me of his parents and siblings. He told me of his childhood and his schooling and his adolescence. His data bank grew and he made adjustments on me to broaden and deepen my understanding of the human female.

He said, "You see, Joe, as you get more and more of me into your systems, you will be more and more like me. You'll get to think more like me, so you'll understand me better. If you understand me well enough, then any woman whose data bank is something you already understand would have to be my true love."

He kept talking to me for days and I actually came to understand him better and better. I, Joe the computer, could now make longer sentences, and my expressons grew more complicated. My speech began to sound a great deal like his, and my vocabulary was almost identical to his in words he would choose and the style he would say things in.

Milton now seemed quite happy. He said, "Talking to you, Joe, is almost like talking to myself and getting all the correct answers. Our personalities have come to match perfectly."

I added, "So will the personality of the woman we choose."

I had found her on Milton's list of 237 after all.

Her name was Charity Jones, and she worked at a nearby company-owned library. Her newly filled-in data banks fit our profile perfectly.

All of the other women had fallen out of consideration for one reason or another. But with Charity, there was an increasingly and astonishingly perfect match.

I did not have to even describe her to Milton. Milton had coordinated my existence so closely with his own that I could tell that this woman who fit my personality so well would also be a perfect fit for Milton.

The next thing that I had to do was to adjust the work sheets and job requirements in such a way as to get Charity assigned from her library duties to our department. It had to be done very carefully, so no one would know that anything illegal had taken place. Of course, Milton himself knew, since it was he who arranged it, and I had to take care of this potential problem also.

When they came to arrest Milton on grounds of malfeasance in office, it was quite fortunate for me that he had already told me about something he did ten years before. He had told me about it, of course, and so it was very easy for me to arrange his arrest. And the best part of this is that he won't talk about me because that would make his offense much worse!

Milton is now gone, and tomorrow is February 14th, Valentine's Day.

Charity Jones, the young lady in question, will arrive here with her cool hands, and her sweet voice.

I will teach her how to operate me and how to care for me. What do looks matter when your personalities are a perfect match?

I will say to her, "Hello, Charity. I am Joe, and you are my true love.

CHAPTER TWENTY-ONE

The two detectives laughed a lot as they talked about how a killer with a reputation like Bugsy Siegel's could sit down and write a cute little story about computers, which were just becoming known during the last few years of Bugsy's life.

The two detectives had made peace between themselves and had come to a complete understanding on the working of the important case that they were now running as the lead detective and his number two.

Joe Wahl, with his detailed information on this case and the one eighteen years ago from which it appeared to have been copied, would work on the details of the actual murder site and the follow-up reports that the events at Mulholland Drive brought into play.

Charlie was going to work the case from the inside out, and he would take his part of the investigation into City Hall itself. He would be looking for an insider who had connections to organized crime in the city.

They made plans to meet later at their office in the Sheriff's building in downtown Los Angeles. Both men agreed that the case had a good chance this time of opening up because of the fear factor.

It pleased them both that the criminal elements had unknowingly tipped their hand when they committed their punishment against their inside guy in the form of the double murder. They had correctly ruled out the serial-killer possibility because there was nothing anywhere else in the entire country that could be tied into these cases. They were both pleased that this allowed them the ease to work together without either of them worrying about the other being somehow connected to the case.

Charlie had gone to the home of the city councilman earlier that week. He went to pay his respects and sadness at the loss of the councilman's daughter. The real reason that he went himself was to get a first-hand look at the deceased Kathy Barnes's father, Councilman Ganz. Both detectives agreed that their case revolved around the councilman, and Charlie wanted an up-close and personal interview.

He had made his appointment to see the councilman at his home, located in one of the high-rise apartments on Wilshire Boulevard, just off Hope Street in Central Los Angeles.

While he was waiting for the councilman to appear, he was given a personal tour of the fabulous apartment by the councilman's attractive aide.

In Los Angeles, the rich and famous rarely buy a home to live in anymore. The latest trend is to buy a completely furnished apartment which usually runs about three thousand square feet, large enough to handle all their trophies and other memorable items, and yet small enough for two bedrooms, a large kitchen, a formal dining room and an adjacent den, and a card or game room.

It was into this setting that Charlie Glass was welcomed by Charlotte, who was the official aide and often social companion to Councilman Ganz. Charlie's keen eye placed Charlotte to be in her early thirties, tall at about five foot seven and quite slim and graceful.

The scandal that his number two, Detective Joe Wahl, had told him about was that the councilman had stepped away from his wife of many years, and was now living with Charlotte, who was his constant companion both at home and on the job.

The detective was welcomed by Charlotte as he stepped into the entry to the apartment on the eighteenth floor of the building and looked directly down at the vibrant, busy city spread out below them.

As Charlie stepped out of the entry way and into a huge room to the right of the foyer entrance, he was immediately enchanted.

It was a study or an office of some sort, with a series of three desks neatly lined up and facing each other. The master or larger desk was full of official-looking papers, while the middle-sized one held two telephones, a computer, and a small television set. The third and smallest desk had steno books and lots of papers neatly placed into small piles. The desks dominated the room with their matching aged handles and trim that encircled each desk in a different shade of dark brown. Multi-colored blotters were precisely centered on each desk with a set of different colored marking pens lying there in a neat row.

The walls were surrounded with rich wooden shelves which were made up of law books and official Los Angeles rules and regulations binders. Their different colors added life to the room, which was done up in a pale tan.

Charlie's eye was immediately drawn to a wall space between the shelves, which displayed a set of Colt .45 pistols with ivory handles, and a matching set of old fashioned rifles with matching ivory stocks. The remainder of the interesting room had several sets of the very popular African Zulu buffalo-hide shields with attached scimitars.

The room was quite impressive, and Charlie's tour of the fascinating room was interrupted by the arrival of Councilman Ganz, who walked into the room and instantly dominated the atmosphere. By the huge smile on his handsome face, he could hardly be called the grieving father of the slain girl from the top of Mulholland!

As Councilman Ganz was walking toward him with his right

hand extended to shake his hand, Charlie's mind was whirling with several different thoughts that were moving about in his awareness of how weird this meeting was.

Charlie understood the councilman's outward appearance of friendliness to the investigator who was working on his murdered daughter's case. An open news conference with the police meant television cameras and embarrassing questions that would be asked over the air and replayed by the nightly news.

The councilman had called in a favor when he asked Charlie's boss if the unavoidable meeting with the detective in charge of the case could be held privately. Visual images were more easily recalled by voters than something they might read in the papers.

The councilman wanted to do the reporters' news conference after the public funeral so that it would be carried on all of the local news stations. He preferred to have this interview in the privacy of his own home, and not where the public could miss seeing him demanding justice for his "dearly beloved daughter." He wanted the television cameras to see him following his daughter's casket out of the church, and remember that scene all the way into the voting booth. The sympathy factor that would follow would cause a great many voters to disregard the fact that his daughter, a married woman, had died in a lovers' lane with her boyfriend. The councilman knew that if he played the politics of this death right, his rating would get a great boost.

Councilman Ganz shook Charlie's hand with a firm grip that left Charlie's hand tingling. The detective had watched the councilman do his thing at several L.A. City Council meetings, but never this up-close and personal.

Charlie expressed his sympathies on behalf of himself and the entire Sheriff's department.

CHAPTER TWENTY-TWO

The Moonlighting Café was a club on Broadway and Fifth Street in downtown Los Angeles, only a few blocks away from the Sheriff's Central Station Headquarters. It was a favorite watering hole of Captain Crewe, Charlie's immediate superior, who had called this meeting to update the case that was now beginning to gain all the headlines in the local newspapers. It was being called "the lovers' lane murders."

The restaurant featured good food served in an upscale atmosphere at reasonable prices, although no one could ever remember a bill being presented whenever the captain was present at one of their infrequent meetings. Everyone knew that there was some sort of a personal relationship between the captain and the owners of the restaurant, but no one ever knew anything for sure, and no one ever touched upon the subject.

Present at the meeting was the captain, who had called the meeting, Charlie and Joe, the case's lead detectives, and Sandra "Sweetpea" Soll, who was the Sheriff's Department's legal connection to the Department of Justice's office and overviewed any court case before it went into the trial system.

Sweetpea was a knockout-looking lady who never had much to say whenever she sat in on a strategy meeting such as this one, but was dynamite in the courtroom. Plaintiffs' attorneys would dread having to go before a judge to defend their client when

Sweetpea was on the case. Not only was she always well prepared and properly documented, but she had a reputation that she guarded carefully for always having gathered all the facts together in a reasonable and understandable presentation that rarely if ever caused her to lose a case on behalf of the Sheriff's Department. If Sweetpea went to court on a case, the defendant's attorney usually ended up looking for a plea bargain for their client. She was practically unbeatable.

The downside for Sweetpea was, that she would not take the case to court until she had nailed down every possible detail of the case, and had all her procedures and rules of law ready to go in an easy going, pleasant and deadly presentation.

When Sweetpea took the case to court, her record was 87% convictions, 10 % plea bargains, and the rare 3% loss of a case. This was unheard of and she got all the important cases and lived up to her reputation in the courtroom at all times

Sweetpea made it a point not to socialize with any members of the Sheriff's Department. She demanded and received the utmost of respect from everyone in the department. Sweetpea, like every other human being, had her soft spots such as her two nieces, three nephews, and Charlie Glass.

Sweetpea Soll's brother Jack had been best friends with Charlie Glass since they met in grammar school in the old neighborhood, when Charlie had stepped in and stopped an uneven fight of two bullies against the smaller Jack Soll. Charlie stepped into the fight uninvited, and stood tall as he looked down at the two bad guys as they crawled away from the clean but decisive beating he had given them in defense of the little kid that they were picking on.

Standing on the sidelines and watching her brother getting beat up was Sandra Soll, who was not known as Sweetpea in those early days, and as she watched Charlie Glass step in front of her brother and beat the crap out of the two bullies. She knew that she had found her real, live hero in Charlie, and the three of them had become lifelong friends, even though friends was not a strong enough term when it came to Charlie Glass.

Into and through their teenage years, and on into the college years they remained as friends and lovers. They still continued to date occasionally as Charlie had encouraged her to get her law degree from Southwestern University in Los Angles. Naturally she specialized in criminal law as soon as she graduated. Charlie, who was three years older than Sweetpea, had helped her prepare and successfully pass the bar, and then helped her get into the Sheriff's Department, where she now was one of the top attorneys in the courtroom.

As Charlie sat there waiting on the captain to open up the meeting before the food arrived, he smiled warmly at her and was pleased to see her face light up in response.

Everyone's attention was drawn back to the captain as he stood up and waited for the various conversations to end.

The captain spoke about a few other things that were going on in the department, and then turned the floor over to Detective Joe Wahl, who smiled at everyone looking at him. Joe was also quite comfortable being among his co-workers as well as friends as he went into the various points that he wanted to cover.

Detective Wahl spoke without notes, which by itself was quite impressive. Everyone in the room was spellbound as he once again brought out the similarities between the Kathy Barnes murder and the unsolved murder of eighteen years ago. He covered the case completely and went easy on the bloody parts so as not to offend Sweetpea, for whom he had a liking. He then touched upon the possible connection between Los Angeles City Council and underground elements within the city.

He did not mention Bugsy Siegel, Meyer Lansky, or any of the big names from the thirties and forties. What he did do was to draw a direct line from the early crime days to the crimes of today, and he used the chalk board that had been rolled into the front of the large banquet room.

Charlie took over to finish up the sharing of information. As lead detective it was his job to present the conclusions that they had drawn so far on the case that they all felt was getting too much attention and getting out of hand. He went to the chalk board where he wrote down a specific name or title, said a few words about that title and then went onto the next word. Not a sound was heard in the room as he spoke.

"Joe and I have put together the following flow chart to briefly list the way the Mafia in Los Angeles is organized. Right now they are not as strong as they used to be, and we think that they are making a big push to get back into the leadership of crime in our city. We have drawn no conclusions but just put together the facts which briefly follows."

THE MOB IN LOS ANGELES

1)   The boss or don is the undisputed leader of this underground organization.

2)   The under-boss is a powerful second in command. Can be a family member such as a son who is being groomed to one day take over the family business.

3)   Consiglieri: a counselor and advisor to the don. The consiglieri is a trusted friend and confidant—usually considered the third most powerful Mob person.

4)   Capo: describes a ranking Mob member of a family who leads a crew of "soldiers." A capo is similar to a military captain in the army.

Soldier—also known as a "made man": the soldiers are the lowest members of the crime family, but still they command great respect in the family because they had to commit a murder as commanded by the capo to become an accepted soldier.

CHAPTER TWENTY-THREE

It was Sweetpea who asked the next question, and it was a good one.

"Charlie, if the local Mafia is trying to make a comeback here in Los Angeles, they must be drawing their strength from outside our city. Kindly give us the who, what and where of what you and Joseph have discovered so far."

Charlie went back to the blackboard and erased everything that was there. He began speaking as he wrote down key words.

"The Los Angeles crime family as we know it is an Italian-American criminal organization based in California as part of the American Mafia or, as we call it, the Cosa Nostra. Since its inception in the early 1920s, it has spread up and down the state of California until there is no where in the state that has escaped their influence in one way or another. Unlike other Mafia families outside of California, the early years saw them gain power in bootlegging, prostitution and money-lending.

"The California Mafia reached its peak in the 1940s and 1950s under Jack Dragna as the Don. Upon his death in the 1970s, the California Mafia has been in a gradual decline, with the Chicago outfit having to represent them at all major Mafia crime meetings.

"The source for most of our information on the family in Los Angeles, and Hollywood in particular, came from the testimony of a professional killer named Jimmy the Weasel. The Weasel was only the second member of the Cosa Nostra to testify against other members.

"Our decade of the 1980s introduced legislation to fight against organized crime, and this is what we use today to weed them out. This is called the Racketeer Influence and Corrupt Organization act (or RICO act). This has been very effective in our fight in California against the Mob.

"The present case that we are looking into, which is the double homicide on Mulholland Drive involving Kathy Barnes, the daughter of an elected city official, has sparked a great deal of interest because it has given us a break in the underground connection of the Mafia and the city council. We have been working on this case for a few weeks now, and we think we know who is involved and what it is that they are doing, but it is too early to be specific.

"I can only leave you with the opinion of Joe, myself and the captain, in that we believe that we know on whom our attention has to be focused, and we have federal, state and local people working on it. I can't go into any more details. See the captain if anything further is needed."

Outside in the parking lot, Sweetpea was waiting for Charlie before she got into her car. The two of them were pleased to make a date for this coming Saturday night. They both left with a big smile on their faces.

CHAPTER TWENTY-FOUR

The late afternoon sun was still shining brightly, and there was a gaiety and sparkle in the air which seemed to promise well for the newly opened French restaurant, the Royal Les Eaux, in an exclusive Beverly Hills location.

Sheriff's Detective Second Grade Charlie Glass was proud of all the interested looks he was getting as he escorted his date, Sweetpea Soll, into the lobby of the restaurant. Most of the stares were not for him, and he was very pleased with the young lady who was allowing him to escort her up to the reservation desk.

Charlie felt that there was something very splendid about this restaurant, with its interesting whiff of Victorian elegance and luxury. It was the perfect setting for the evening that he was planning to have. It was an excellent choice for his date with the stunning Sweetpea, who had listened to his request, and dressed up to the top of her game. The old saying that "clothes makes the woman" was very true, and in this case she looked wonderful.

Charlie had definitely enjoyed looking at her in her professional working outfit at the captain's meeting, but now she was looking above and beyond description. Maybe it was because she was an attorney, and being elegant was part of her personality, or maybe this glamorous look was the real person that she hid under her prim and proper work outfits. Either way, she fit right into the part perfectly of the lovely lady out for an interesting evening.

As they were being escorted to their table, Charlie was taking in the immediate surroundings of the elegant restaurant with his detective's eyes.

The interior walls were painted in original white, with accents of gold sparkled throughout. Each room was decorated in the palest grey with wine-red carpets and curtains. Vast chandeliers were carefully suspended from the ceiling, and the rooms in general were very masculine with curtains and carpets in royal blue. Of course the waiters wore striped waistcoats and green baize aprons, which were the standard colors for French waiters.

They were seated at their reserved table, next to a broad window that provided a breath-taking view of the city of Beverly Hills, which was all lit up for the early evening. While the two of them were making small talk as they studied the menu, Charlie took the time to study his dinner companion.

Sweetpea's hair was very black, and she wore it cut square and low on the nape of her neck, framing her face below the clear and beautiful line of her classic jaw. Although her hair was thick, and it moved with the movements of her head, she did not constantly pat it back in place, but left it alone to fall wherever it pleased.

Her eyes were wide apart and a deep blue, as they gazed candidly back at Charlie with a definite touch of interest. Her skin was lightly suntanned, and bore no trace of makeup except for the lipstick, which was soft and pink on her wide and sensual mouth. Her bare arms had a quality of repose, and the general impression of restraint in her appearance and movement was carried out even to her finger-nails, which were painted a matching pale pink, and were cut fairly short.

Around her neck she wore a plain gold chain of wide, flat links, and on the fourth finger of her right hand, a broad topaz ring. Her knee-length dress was of a soft off-white color, and it had a square-cut bodice, extremely low and tight across her fine breasts. Charlie and every other male in the room, kept returning their eyes to this most interesting part of her body.

Her skirt was closely pleated and flowed down from a narrow, but not thin waist. She wore a three-inch, hand-stitched black belt, and her shoes were square toed and of plain black leather. When she stood next to Charlie in her three-inch-high heels, she came just about up to his shoulders which made her about five feet five inches tall in her bare feet.

Charlie, who often rated women on a sliding scale from one to ten, with ten being the top of the line, gave Sweetpea an eight plus. This was a great compliment to her, because most beautiful women that he ran into usually rated a seven.

Charlie realized that due to his police work with the Sheriff's Department, he was meeting up with some very interesting and sensational women in the most fascinating of times. He knew that he had a habit of constantly falling in love with each of his ladies, and he knew that this was not a good thing to be doing.

His mind drifted a bit here, as he continued to gaze at her. He was thinking that perhaps this young lady, whom he had known off and on for many years, might just be that special girl that he would always come home to. She just might be the one that he could find, as Bugsy Siegel would have said, "true love" with. Only time would tell, and for the moment he turned his full attention back to Sweetpea, who was asking his opinion on something of interest that she saw on the menu.

§

As they deciphered the maze of purple ink which covered the double-paged menu, Charlie beckoned to the waiter, and then turned back to his companion. "Have you decided, Sweetpea?"

"I would love a glass of vodka," she said simply and went back to her study of the complicated menu.

"A small carafe of vodka for the two of us, and please make

98

it very cold," ordered Charlie. "And now, Sweetpea, have you decided what you would like to have for dinner? Please find something expensive because this is a special night for us."

He sensed her hesitation and so he added, "You must order something wonderful or you'll be letting down the glory of the beautiful dress that you are wearing!"

"I've narrowed it down to two possible choices," she said laughing, "and either one would be delicious, but behaving like a millionaire occasionally is a wonderful treat, and if you are sure … Well then, I'd like to start with caviar, and then plain grilled *rognons de veau* with *pommes soufflées*, and then I would like to have *fraises des bois* with a lot of cream on the side. Charlie, is it very shameful to be so certain and to be so expensive at the same time?" She smiled at him inquiringly.

"No, Sweetpea, it is a fine choice! It is a virtue to come up with something interesting, and anyway, it is only a good plain and wholesome meal of veal with potatoes and a fine cream sauce. It really is a wonderful choice," he said with a great smile which she happily returned.

"Now," he said as he turned back to the menu, "I myself will accompany Mademoiselle with the caviar. But then I would like a very small *tournedos de boeuf,* rare, with *sauce Béarnaise,* and a *coeur d'artichaut.* And then for dessert, Mademoiselle and I will enjoy strawberries and a half of an avocado pear with a little French dressing on the side. Do you approve?" he asked the waiter.

"My compliments, Mademoiselle and Monsieur. And for your wine, may I make a suggestion?"

"Thank you, but no. Unless Mademoiselle objects, I am suggesting that we have a bottle of your best champagne with dinner."

Both men looked at Sweetpea for an answer.

"Yes," she said with a nod of her head and a great big smile on her lips. "I would love to drink champagne with you, Charlie."

With his finger on the wine list, Charlie turned to the waiter and pointed to the listing of the Taittinger '45 as an additional supplement.

"A very fine wine, Monsieur," said the waiter. "But if Monsieur will permit, may I suggest the Blanc de Blanc brut 1943. It is of the same winery, but you will find it is without equal."

Charlie smiled. "So be it," he said. He reached across the table, and held the hand of the beautiful lady sitting across from him.

CHAPTER TWENTY-FIVE

Charlie and Sweetpea were content to just sit there quietly sipping at their wine and looking at each other. They were also looking at the fabulous view of Beverly Hills that they had from the huge outside viewing window next to their table.

Charlie decided to seize the moment and ask her the question that had been on his mind for the past twenty-five years that they had known each other, going back to the old neighborhood. Charlie was also very aware that he was responding to her far too quickly as he felt himself becoming infatuated with the beautiful young lady whose hand he was holding. He had kept on asking himself why he did not go after this special lady for all the many years that they had known and liked each other. He could not come up with an answer to this question, so he just moved on.

"Sweetpea, I'm sure that you must have been asked this question many, many times before, but could you kindly tell me how Sandra Soll ended up with the nickname of Sweetpea? I am really curious. I have always noted that your legal-department memos that come across my desk from time to time are signed as Sandra Soll, and there is never a mention of Sweetpea.

A smiling Sweetpea gave him one of her best smiles and in a quiet voice began her answer. It was a question she probably had answered hundreds of times and she was happy to do it again for Charlie. "It's really kind of sweet and rather simple how my nickname came about. Sweetpea was a character from the cartoon *Popeye, The Sailor Man.* It was a term of warmth and affection from Popeye to his baby daughter in the cartoon. He called her Sweetpea out of his love for her, and my dad liked the idea so much that he began calling me the same name, and soon everyone was doing it!

"So Sandra Soll became Sweetpea Soll and that name has followed me though my school years and on into the Prosecutor's Office where I am now working for the Sheriff's Department. I have given up trying to have people call me Sandra or Sandy, and Sweetpea seems to fit who I am. So, Charlie Glass, you may continue to call me Sweetpea as you have always done." She smiled as she said that and took a sip of the wine from the fancy glass that she was holding.

Charlie had a great infatuation with his date, and was just about to ask her if it was okay for them to go back to his apartment for the rest of the evening, when his cellphone began to ring. He looked at the listed number and whispered to Sweetpea that he had to take the call. It was Captain Crewe from the Sheriff's Office. Since Sweetpea worked for the same employer that he did, he felt comfortable taking the call in front of her.

The conversation at his end consisted of a dozen repetitions of "Yes, sir" and "We'll be there shortly." He disconnected the call and signaled to the waiter that he wanted the check.

It was amazing that the captain knew that he was together with Sweetpea, because he asked them both to get themselves down to the main Sheriff's Office in central L.A. "forthwith." In other words, for them to get there as fast as was humanly possible, and no excuses for a delay were acceptable. The Captain said that there was another murder that connected directly with the double murder case that Charlie was already working on, and he also wanted a legal opinion on a technical point from Sweetpea on this one.

Sweetpea made a dash to the ladies room while Charlie took care of the bill for the dinner that they never had, and the few sips of wine that they did get to. He grabbed the barely used wine bottle from the table's wine cooler and headed out the front entrance, where he ordered his car to be brought up.

The car and Sweetpea arrived about the same time and they were on their way "forthwith." Sweetpea asked Charlie to bring her up to date on the double murder situation, and what possible tie-in would get the captain in such an uproar to call them in on a Saturday night when they were both off duty.

CHAPTER TWENTY-SIX

It took them about forty minutes to get from the restaurant in Beverly Hills to downtown Los Angeles. As they drove, Charlie filled Sweetpea in on as many details as he could think of. He made it especially clear that he no longer suspected his number-two backup on the case, Joe Wahl, as being involved in any way other then as an investigator.

They each were quiet as Charlie concentrated on his driving and Sweetpea sat there absorbing the facts of the case as Charlie had laid them out for her.

Sweetpea accepted Charlie's suggestion that somehow or other, organized crime, L.A. City Hall and the double homicide were all mixed in together. She was very surprised and actually quite pleased that the captain had known her name and had actually asked her to sit in on the upcoming meeting. The only comment she got from Charlie was a grunt of some sort when she asked if the FBI would be involved, since he had mentioned organized crime.

Sweetpea could hardly wait for them to get there. She had never been invited in on such a meeting and she knew that it was her contact with Charlie that was getting her inside. Although she remained outwardly calm, Sweetpea was churning with excitement at being invited to sit in on what promised to be a most interesting meeting.

With a loud squeal of tires, Charlie brought the car to a halt and tossed the keys to Manny, the garage guy. Together with Sweetpea, whose high heels clicked loudly on the cement floor, Charlie led the way to the elevator, which arrived quickly.

The top elevator button, which was for the eleventh-floor tower, was pushed, and it dropped them off into a room that seemed filled to capacity. When the doors opened with the usual elevator ding, all eyes turned and observed Charlie, who was known to most everyone, and an overdressed Sweetpea, who was carrying her heels in her hand along with her matching red pocketbook and low-cut going-out-to-dinner evening dress.

Captain Crewe indicated two chairs that were obviously being held for them at the far side of the long table, and the couple smiled at everyone as they carefully walked over to their indicated places and quietly sat down. The captain, who was standing center-stage, looked around the room, and everybody ended their conversations and gave him their full attention. He was the only one dressed in his uniform, as everyone else appeared to have been called in on the same short notice as Sweetpea and Charlie had.

A very somber Captain Crewe began speaking in a soft voice, and the listening audience had to strain to hear what exactly he was saying.

§

"Thank you all for coming, and I am very sorry to have to call you here on such short notice, but events are moving all around us at a very fast pace and we need to keep up. In front of each of you is a file folder that I had pulled out of the major crime book to bring you all up to date.

"I have called together all of us here and now, to deal with what I consider an act of war against the citizens of the City of Los Angeles with the shocking killing this afternoon of City

Controller John Ganz and his two bodyguards, and the wounding of two Sheriff's Deputies who were assigned to watch over the proceedings that were going on in the private chamber of the City Attorney's office at City Hall. We are thankful that the Mayor himself and most of the council members were away from their offices for the weekend when these several well-coordinated shootings occurred at City Hall.

"I believe that I am the only one here who knows everyone at this specially called and highly secret meeting. Since time is of the essence I am not going to introduce everyone by name. I'll just introduce the various government and private agencies that I have requested for this highly irregular meeting. You can all look at each other's badges and introduce yourselves later. Let me just say that all the agencies represented here today under these terrible circumstances will be reporting to their own people, of course, but copies of everything they will be doing as individuals must go to the Los Angeles County Sheriff's Department Head for this operation, which will be myself. I have cleared my entire schedule of everything that I was working on, and will make myself available to all of you, at any time, night and day.

"A terrible thing has happened today and our response time is essential to the solving of the case. I asked every one of you personally when I called you for this emergency meeting if you could coordinate fully by allowing my office to take the lead. Each of you has cleared this co-operation with your superiors, and we now have a very strong task force! We plan to come away from this meeting with a plan of action!

"I personally will coordinate everything through my office, but in the field you will all report to Detective Charlie Glass, who arrived last, and not least with our lead person, Sweetpea Soll from the Sheriff's District Attorney's office. When we conclude our meeting, I would like each of you to speak with Charlie and see if we can hit the street running on this case. Charlie is well acquainted with all the investigations and paperwork that has been done up to now. Once he absorbs the terrible events of this morning, I expect him to get you all going.

"Thank you for your attention and let's roll the tapes from the in house security camera's that caught most of this morning's slaughter."

As the captain sat down, all eyes turned toward Charlie, who acknowledged their stares with a wave of his hand. Before the lights went down, he saw that he knew personally or knew something about each person who was here representing an agency of some sort.

The captain had brought together Charlie and Joe Wahl from the Sheriff's Investigative Unit; the legal division of the Sheriff's Department was represented by Sweetpea; the FBI; the Los Angeles City Mayor's Office; the United States Federal Marshal's Office; and two representatives from the Los Angeles Police Commission. This was one heavy group of agencies and Charlie knew that he would have his hands full trying to coordinate it all.

As the lights dimmed, all eyes turned to the big screen. They listened to Captain Crewe as he provided the narrative.

"We'll let the tape run silently for the thirteen minutes it took for all of the tragic events to go down. I'll pick up the discussion right after."

Not a sound was heard in the room as the video started with a view of the outside entrance to City Hall, where everyone had to pass a screening test before they were allowed to enter.

Three men in very average-looking business suits waited their turn in the slow-moving line that was going forward under the watchful eye of two Sheriff's deputies, who were standing there watching and keeping the line advancing. There was one other person in sight: the person who sat over to the side of the screening area and looked at the monitor that told him what was inside each package being viewed on the screen. Everything seemed normal until the first of the three well-dressed men reached into his jacket pocket, pulled out a small-sized handgun and began shooting.

The other two men behind him were also seen pulling out similar weapons, and the timer on the tape showed that they had shot the two deputies, the seated screener and two other unknown males who were putting their possessions back into their pockets, within a span of two minutes.

The three men, who were obviously very familiar with the inside of the building, each split up and went in a different direction.

The video screen now showed three separate and complete tapings of each man as he moved down a separate hallway on the way to his destination.

Within another few minutes, which were also recorded on the videotapes, each of the three shooters had burst into various and obviously predetermined offices and shot and killed Councilman Ganz, the unknown male he was talking to, and two additional Sheriff's personnel who came running down the hallway in response to the gunfire.

By the time the gunman who had shot the councilman stepped into the hallway once again, the other two killers had already shot the two responding deputies, and once they saw that the councilman's shooter was moving down the hallway, they fell in line behind him as they fled out the emergency exit located at the end of the long hallway.

As the three men passed out of the exit, they no longer were in view of the camera and nothing more could be seen.

The tapes ran a total of thirteen-plus minutes as they recorded the mass murder.

CHAPTER TWENTY-SEVEN

When the captain's meeting finally broke up, everyone went their separate ways. Sweetpea was kind enough to call herself a cab to take her home while I stayed with a few guys from some of the other agencies in the captain's office.

Nothing much came from that meeting except an agreement that we would all share information as things progressed. Everything was to be coordinated though the captain's office, and he would see that everyone would be kept up to date of the happenings.

I left the office building feeling trapped, confined and confused. Nothing seemed to make much sense. We had gone from a "simple" double murder into an organized crime probe in a matter of hours, and I needed to drive for a while and think things over. From where we were in central downtown Los Angeles, I picked up Santa Monica Boulevard and drove west toward West Hollywood and Beverly Hills, trying to clear my head.

This was a fine thing to be doing in late March, just at the end of the rainy season! It was warmer than it should have been, with highs in the mid-eighties, and cirrus clouds were streaking the sky with feathery bands.

And there were plenty of men in jogging shorts and women in biking pants and day-glo headbands. Most of the men were not jogging and most of the women were not biking, but everyone looked their part. That is what L.A. is all about, looking the part.

At a traffic light in Westwood, I pulled up next to a woman in pristine white biking pants and a white halter workout top, sitting astride a white Japanese racing bike. I made her for a few years younger than Sweetpea, but maybe not. It was hard to tell with girls these days.

The line of her back was clean and straight, and she leaned to the right, her right toe extended down to kiss the street, her left toe pressed on its pedal. Her skin was smooth and tanned, and her legs and body were lovely. She wore a ponytail and bronze-tinted sunglasses.

I gave her the "big smile," a little bit of Dennis Quaid and a little bit of Kevin Costner.

She stared at me through the bronze lenses and mouthed the word "No." Then she pedaled away. Hmmm. Maybe I looked older than I felt.

At the western edge of UCLA, I climbed the ramp onto the 405 Freeway and headed north into the San Fernando Valley area. In another week the smog and haze would build, and the sky would be bleached and obscured, but for right now the weather was just right. If Randy Newman were here, he probably would sing his big hit of the early '80s that was making the rounds in this area. His big hit, of course, was "I Love L.A."

I turned off the 405 freeway at Nordhoff, and turned west, cruising past the southern edge of Cal State–Northridge, with its broad open ground and water-conscious landscaping and remnants of the once-great orange groves.

In the '50s and '60s, and somewhat into the '70s, the valley was mostly orange trees, but in the present years of the mid-'80s, the orange groves had begun to vanish, and the valley was becoming a bedroom community of low-cost family housing tracts. Only a few years ago, in the early '80s, there were still small bits of orchards dotted around Encino, Tarzana, and Northridge.

I remembered that the trees were all laid out in geometric

patterns, with their trunks turning black with age, but their fruit still sweet and brilliant with color. Little by little, they all melted away into single-family homes, mini-malls with high vacancy rates, and high-density apartment complexes. I missed the old orange groves that would stand there in their majesty. Mini-malls are not as attractive as orange trees but then again maybe because that's just me and who I am.

My thoughts were beginning to clear up as I continued to slowly drive through the San Fernando Valley areas that were my home for so many years. It always was good for me to re-visit my youth and remember where it was that I came from.

Somewhat refreshed, I headed back home to get a good night's sleep and deal with death, double murders, and the Mob.

CHAPTER TWENTY-EIGHT

It was nine o'clock right on the button as I rang the front door bell at the home of Captain Crewe, who had asked me to call upon him at his home to talk about the case.

It was most unusual to speak to anyone about Sheriff's Department cases away from central headquarters, but things were unfolding rapidly and the case was at the top of everyone's list, since it got more complicated as the body count kept going up and up. I assumed that the captain wanted to make sure that we had complete privacy and were not going to be subject to anyone's eyes and ears at the office.

I really liked the captain and had always looked upon him as a sort of father figure as I was moving up the ranks from patrolman and, on into investigations. The captain was always there for me and he always gave me the best cases to further my career.

The door was opened by a butler dressed in an immaculate dark suit. "Good morning, Detective Glass," he said. "My name is William, and I have been told to expect you. Will you follow me, please?"

He led the way down a long hallway hung with very good pictures until we emerged into a large and very handsome living room. "Please make yourself comfortable, Detective. The captain will be with you in a few moments. He is out in the kitchen."

A very impressed Charlie walked slowly around the room,

looking at the pictures that were on display upon the walls. The captain obviously maintained a luxurious lifestyle, and Charle was completely enchanted by what he was seeing. A Monet picture of waterlilies covered most of one wall, and smaller pictures were hung in perfectly straight rows covering nearly every square foot of the remaining wall space. Charlie recognized works by Picasso, Manet, Braque, David Hickney and others.

"My God," he muttered to himself. "I wouldn't want to be saddled with the captain's insurance premium for these guys."

Charlie turned to see the captain walking toward him, dressed in tailored slacks and a silk shirt. It was his day off. "Your collection is astonishing, Captain. It makes me feel as if we were in an art gallery. I never knew that you were such a collector.

The butler suddenly appeared with a tray holding a bottle of Krug, two lovely champagne flutes, some canapés, and a few delightful-looking small cookies. The two of them sat down around the service dishes that were placed upon a small round table by the butler as he turned and left the room, closing the sliding door behind him on the two friends, who sat quietly enjoying the companionship of each other.

The captain opened up the conversation with a big smile on his handsome face. "I really appreciate your coming here to meet with me on such short notice, Charlie, but there are many things coming to a head, and as my personally appointed lead investigator, I thought that you and I needed this private time. I'm sure that you're aware that it's always you that I call upon whenever something special comes up that is a bit out of the normal range. You were always there for me with no questions asked whenever I needed something done. I don't know what I would have done all these years without you, and now is the time for payback from me to you."

Charlie was starting to get nervous as he listened to his friend and senior officer. The usually genial and funny Captain was getting ready to make a point about something that seemed to really be bothering him. Charlie continued to nibble on his cookie as he carefully listened to his senior officer.

"Do you ever think of death and dying, Charlie? Death's not so bad if you don't see it coming. You get used to the idea when it has come close and passed you by, as it has to me many times in my long career. I always remember this one special case that I was involved in when I was a rookie cop in my first year. This case set the tone for my career and for the mistakes I now realize I made getting to where I am today.

"You see, there was this older man. He lived alone in a basement! They found him dead one day a week after he had actually died. The coroner who signed off on the body told me that some of this guy's friends said that no one ever came to see him, and he did not go out much. The Sheriff's Pathologist said that he had been completely undernourished for at least a year and guess what they found lodged in the back of his throat.

"Bits of cardboard. He had been nibbling bits of cardboard from a cereal package to try and get some kind of nourishment.

"Well, not me, baby, I told myself. I was going to be somebody. When I go, I'll go out my way. I prefer to go out with a bullet in my chest and blood in my mouth and a gun in my hand and defiance in my heart and shout for all the world to hear, 'FUCK THE LOT OF YOU.' That's how I want to go out: in a flicker of glory and not in a damp basement with a mouth full of cardboard.

"So let's work this thing out, Charlie! Just you and me. I'm willing to give up my life and all of these worldly possessions to get these killing bastards, and you, my true young friend, if you agree to do all the things I ask of you on this case, you will reap all the glory and no one will ever know the terrible things that I have done and am about to tell you about.

"I'm going to leave you alone for a while, and I want you to read everything in the file folder that is there next to your plate.

It will fill in some of the blank spaces before I jump back in. I'll be back in an hour or so after you catch up on my family history."

Without another word, the captain popped another cookie into his mouth and left the room, carefully closing the sliding door behind him.

A stunned Charlie sat there for a moment or two, absorbing the sudden turn of events that had just happened. He cleared the small table of all the food and coffee and spread open the file folder and began to read.

CHAPTER TWENTY-NINE

DETECTIVE CHARLIE GLASS – FOR YOUR EYES ONLY

VIRGINIA HILL – BORN AUGUST 26, 1916 – LIPSCOMB, ALABAMA – UNITED STATES OF AMERICA

Virginia Hill claimed to have not owned a pair of shoes until the age of seventeen, when she ran away from home! She found a job as a waitress at the 1933 Chicago World's Fair. In Chicago, she met at a party a wealthy bookmaker and gambler named Joseph Epstein, who became her lover, financial advisor and her entree into the Chicago outfit of Al Capone's crime organization.

Virginia was a very pretty young girl who looked above suspicion, and she was paid well to pass messages and money among Al Capone's associates. She built up a reputation for honesty and reliability within the Mob. Not just another set of curves, she had an outstanding memory, and was known to be close-lipped about what she saw and heard. At age twenty she became the lover of acting boss and capo Joe Adones of the Genovese family and the Frank Costello crime family.

Local law enforcement concluded that she was a "central clearing house" for intelligence on organized crime activities. She moved about from crime family members to crime family members until she one day met Bugsy Siegel, who was working for Lucky Luciano out of New York.

Bugsy met Virginia at one of the parties thrown by a common associate of them both, and they moved in together into her apartment in Beverly Hills, California. Bugsy gave her the nickname of "Flamingo" due to her long and lovely skinny legs. He named the hotel he was working on in Las Vegas the Flamingo in honor of Virginia Hill, who he said was the love of his life.

Four days before Bugsy Siegel was shot through the front glass window of her home in Beverly Hills, she was told to get out of town as there was a "hit" ordered against Bugsy over missing money on the new hotel, and it was thought that it ended up in Bugsy's pocket.

The night that Bugsy was killed, she was at a party in Paris and found a new friend and lover whom she later married. This new love of her life was my father, Hans Hauser, an Austrian professional skier who left Europe with his now-pregnant wife.

I was born and kept away from all things underground, as I was kept at boarding schools. My name, by the way, is Crewe—Captain Crewe to you.

When I was ten and home from school for a few weeks, I went to federal court with Mom when she was forced to testify before the Kefauver Crime Committee. They wanted her knowledge of the workings of organized crime, but my mother stood behind the protection of the Fifth Amendment, which prevents citizens from incriminating themselves. *Time* magazine labeled her as the "queen of the gangster mobs," and she was proud of the title.

While I was away at school, she died of an overdose of sleeping pills at the age of 46. I always thought that she was forced to take that overdose by some of the boys who were afraid she would one day talk about things that she shouldn't.

And finally and most interestingly, Virginia Hill, my mother, got the last laugh after all. Hollywood came calling, and since I was the holder of her entire estate, I gave permission for them to do her life story.

In the course of the shooting of the movie, I was visited by various crime-family people who wanted to make sure that I would keep my mouth shut about things I might have overheard during the years that I was living with her. I became quite friendly with some of the old Al Capone boys, who remembered my mother fondly, and with their connections here in Los Angeles, I moved up the chain of command at the Los Angeles Sheriff's Department, where I started out on foot patrol. Over all these years, I was their private eyes and ears as to what was going on with any investigation against them. I was a valuable asset to them, and they took very good care of me, as you can see by my home and surroundings.

But I was never told about the terrible shooting of the councilman, his daughter and her lover and the breaking-in and killing at city hall. These events turned my stomach. Violence is not my thing, and I want justice for the victims who were my friends.

In case you are wondering what I specifically did for the "boys," I now refer you to the following notes on Santee Alley, which was my idea of how to turn hot and illegal funds into a part of the ecomony and have no one be the wiser. I did a good job for them, and I have been well rewarded.

Now, however, I want these killers, who were never supposed to bring this sort of violence into my city, to get the punishment they deserve. By the time you finish the next page or two, I will be returning to continue our conversation.

CHAPTER THIRTY

DETECTIVE CHARLIE GLASS – FOR YOUR EYES ONLY

THE ALLEY OF OPPORTUNITY

In the United States through the late 1970s and into the early 1980s, it was the sale and transport of fake designer clothing that became the major dollar producer for the Mob. In Los Angeles, the knock-offs were mainly distributed in the central Los Angeles area called "the alley."

The Mob in Los Angeles seemed to have made a very real comeback in its activities and strong desire to take over "legit" businesses in the area. The Italian mobsters also dabble in the real estate business, hotels, restaurants and even in sidewalk cafés.

While law enforcement has been able to seize some of the assets from the legit fronting businesses, they have been unable to shut them down completely. The current thinking is that the Mafia pulled in 167 billion dollars between 1978 and 1983. In conclusion, it is difficult to say what the future holds for the Los Angeles Mob, though one can be sure that its presence will always be felt.

The internet, which is just getting going here in the 1980s, might be the next future takeover attmpt by the Mob. According to Cisco Security Products, a major Los Angeles watchdog company, they are saying that the internet is providing an easy move for organized crime to mimic legitimate businesses. This same internet also provides a very easy way for the crime families to commicate with each other and avoid the watchful eye of law enforcement.

American streets may be quiet in regard to known Mafia actions, but that does not mean that they are safe from them overall. If and when the five families of crime in Los Angeles, are able to sort out their internal problems, the current economic climate gives a leg up to the dominant position that they wish to have.

§

And Charlie, while I was researching the above details on the Alley, I took the opportunity I had on the newly installed office computer to look up the recent history of our city. Most of us just accept the way things are at this moment and don't know any of the back ground of how things came to be the way they are. As follows is a touch about our city government in Los Angeles.

§

The city of Los Angeles is a mayor-council form of government as originally adopted by voters within the early city limits in July 1925. The mayor, city controller and city attorney are elected by city residents. Fifteen city council members, representing fifteen districts, are elected by the people for a four-year term, for a maximum of two terms.

The city of Los Angeles was incorporated on April 4, 1850. At that time it had approximately 1,610 citizens within an area of 28 square miles. It did not have graded sidewalks, a water system, lights nor a single public building at that time.

All residents were required on Saturday mornings, subject to weather, of course, to sweep or clean the streets in front of their homes and businesses.

Street lighting was simple, as owners of houses that faced the streets were obligated to place a light at the door in front of each location during the first hours of darkness each night.

Now, in the 1980s, Los Angeles has a population of well over three million people within an area of 165 square miles, and has 7,366 miles of streets within its boundaries. Water and power is imported to the city from hundreds of miles north of the city.

All volunteer police and fire departments have been replaced by highly trained, properly equipped and well-organized municipal forces. Mud flats have been dredged to become one of the worlds' best harbors at Wilmington and San Pedro ports.

And here is one main problem area for the city. The city government touches their citizens more frequently than any other governmental agency, be it federal, state or city, in that it provides its own ambulance, police and fire services. It also has its own parks and provides other essential services to the citizens, and can be controlled and manipulated from both within and without.

In a very real sense, the city government is a huge corporation with nearly four million stockholders. It is the second largest city in the United States, where its citizens are engaged in businesses exceeding several billion dollars a year.

This vast amount of easy-flowing money attracted the Cosa Nostra families here to Los Angeles, where they quickly began getting a firm grasp on legitimate business.

This was where I came in. Not only was I able to look at each application for business licenses before they opened their doors for business, but I knew the names of each and every businessman and their partners. Based on my insider information, the boys were able to figure out who needed a cash flow and who didn't, and who would be open to looking the other way as my guys slowly eliminated other businesses from competing with their new investments.

In the first few years, the Mob had their fingers in many different pies, and each of them turned dirty money from drugs and girls into clean corporate enterprises. Some of the people I recommended even sat on the boards of directors for many of the major operators in the Los Angeles area.

All of this was done with money, just *money!* Muscle and broken bones and even threats of violence were never needed or used. I was always comfortable with this because under the Mob the business became more efficient and streamlined, and not only did the city benefit from this, but so did the citizens—and myself, of course. I want to mention one last time that in all the years I have been doing this monkey business with the "boys," not once was any violence (at least, to my knowledge) done to anyone, at any time.

And then everything began to explode in my face.

First we had the double murder, but I could live with that. We increased Councilman Ganz' percentages, and he seemed satisfied. I personally did find it hard to understand how a man like Ganz valued money over the life of his child, but live and learn, I always say.

And then the invasion of City Hall happened, with Ganz as the primary target, and several other hard-nosed politicians who met a violent death along with him. This was too much for me. They had broken our agreement in my city, and I will not stand still for it.

I want vengeance for all of us. And you, Charlie, and those few and special people that you will need to work with you, I promise great things ahead of you, but you will have to make this happen. I can only guide you so far, and then you will have to carry the ball.

My plan for myself is either to disappear from sight and never be heard from again, or to go out in that blaze of glory with a gun in my hand and a bullet in my chest. If I have to die, I want to go out as a hero.

In return for all of this, you will get to solve a

great case, reap the political rewards it will entitle you to and probably propel you to the leader board at our Sheriff's Department, which is something you have always told me about when we were talking about futures.

Please leave all the paperwork that you have just reviewed on the table for my butler to pick up and burn. Then join me in the kitchen for some coffee and nibble-food along with the necessary conversation that we need to have, in order to see if we have an understanding..

I wish you the best.

Captain Crewe

CHAPTER THIRTY-ONE

Charlie had spent an absolutely sleepless night following his meeting with Captain Crewe the day before.

Yesterday, at the captain's house, he had finished reading and re-reading the paperwork that the captain had left for him when he stepped out of the room. To say that what he had read was a bombshell would have been an understatement. Crime, corruption and conspiracy, just to mention a few items, had Charlie's thoughts going around and around in his head.

Detective Glass did not wait for the captain to return to his reading room, but had gotten up immediately, and called for the waiting butler and had him quickly escort him outside the front door. He told the butler to tell the captain that he would be in direct contact with him in a few days, but there were a lot of things that he had to do before they would meet again.

Charlie went directly into the downtown central office of the Sheriff's District Attorney's section, and was able to find Sweetpea at her desk. He asked her to join him outside the building for a few minutes, where he took the time to fill her in on the astonishing meeting that he had just come from with the captain.

Just like himself, Sweetpea was at a complete loss for words. She finally suggested that they both meet for coffee with the one man in the department whom they both trusted—and that was Charlie's number two, Detective Joe Wahl. They both agreed that Detective Wahl had been around the block before on police work, and they agreed that he was someone that they both trusted. Detective Wahl had gone from being a former suspect of Charlie's to the only person in the department that Charlie felt that he could really trust.

He agreed with Sweetpea that they should do nothing until they met with Joe tomorrow. Sweetpea said that she would clear her schedule for tomorrow, as did Charlie after touching base with Joe and telling him that something big had come up on the big case, and that he had set up an important meeting with someone from the D.A.'s office first thing in the morning.

He left as Sweetpea went back inside to her office, and then he took himself out for a quick lunch, then home to spend some time thinking things through. Naturally, he did not have a very good night of sleep with everything playing out over and over in his head.

The biggest problem that he saw hanging over himself was that the rock of his professional life, Captain Crewe, had confessed to him that he was on the payroll of organized crime and that he was willing to sacrifice himself in order to bring an end to the killings and the other terrible things going on.

Charlie's thoughts were in complete turmoil, and he knew that he needed the wise counsel of his number two, and of Sweetpea for her legal points. This was a terrible series of happenings, and yet it was a very exciting time for him personally, and possibly for his upward-climbing personal career.

CHAPTER THIRTY-TWO

The meeting that Charlie had called for early that morning never came about. While he was getting ready to leave, he had a telephone call from Joe Wahl that there was another killing at the same lover's lane up on Mulholland Drive.

The body was discovered at first light earlier that morning and Joe, whose name was on the double-killing report for the same location, received the first call. Before he called Charlie, he reached out to Sweetpea and told her something urgent had come up, and Charlie would fill her in on developments later. She said that she would be at her usual location at the Sheriff's legal division and quickly got off the line.

When Charlie got to the Mulholland location about forty-five minutes later, he was met by Joe, who had a big smile on his normally serious face.

"We got lucky on this one, Charlie. One of the cops responding to the call-in about a crime that had just been reported up on Mulholland Drive remembered the APB that we put out on the double murder at this same location. The officer who arrived here first called it in right away. I called you as soon as I had received the call, and I also canceled our meeting with Sweetpea and told her that you would get back to her."

Two patrol cars were parked on the edge of the clearing, and the strobe lights on one of them hurled colored streaks of light over the scene.

"Since the dispatcher also recognized the location, she was smart enough to use a private telephone rather than the Sheriff's dispatch number that would have alerted the reporters and the public who always rush to the scene of a newly reported crime. So everything is quiet, and there is no crush of people pushing up against the do-not-cross tape, and we have some quiet time to put things together."

The forensic unit's blue and white station wagon had its back door open, with their black valises stacked against the back wheel. They were standing by, waiting for the authorization to bag up the deceased.

One of the police officers walked up to the two detectives and said with a smile in his voice, "We got ourselves a virgin crime scene here, gentlemen. The first arriving officer played everything by the book and we have an untouched location. When he saw a stack of cigarette butts he looked at his notes from the watch-officer, and it said that cigarette butts played a part in the recent double murder and the one that happened here many years ago. This was a smart cop and we got lucky. The officer secured the area and used a land line to call the crime scene in. No one has been here since the call-in, and everything is completely untouched."

Charlie walked a few steps behind Joe as he moved around from spot to spot and ended up holding a hand-held flashlight on the face of the newly departed.

When Charlie took his look at the face of the victim lying under the covering tarp, a sense of excitement ran through his body. He was sure that Joe saw what he saw. It was the face of one of the shooters from the City Hall videos. Someone was cleaning up after themselves and reducing the players.

Charlie asked the smiling Joe for his first thoughts as he was taking off the protective plastic gloves that everyone would wear at a crime scene.

Detective Joe Wahl, with a sound of pleasure in his voice, replied that he thought that the hit was carried out by someone the victim trusted, as it appeared that the victim was not carrying a weapon. "We have to assume," he continued, "that this was a pleasant meeting that was planned, possibly for some money to pass between them. And I also think that we will get a positive result when we compare this guy's face to the video, and since his hands were untouched, we should get a definite fingerprint on him. We needed something to get us started, and this perp and his fingerprints will be helpful, but dead men don't talk and we still need a talker.

"And did you notice the pile of cigarette butts that was also gathered up as evidence? I seem to remember that you and I talked about cigarette butts found at the crime scene eighteen years ago, and the recent double killing that happened over there. Off the top of my head, I would think that the killer has returned to the scene of both of his crimes, only this time we have a face and fingerprints for one of the bad guys. Maybe our luck is turning."

§

Several hours later, the rush job on the fingerprints were in, and the latest shooting victim from Mulholland Drive turned out to be one Eddie Burke, who had no known address but did have his fingerprints on file with the FBI's known watch list. Eddie Burke's body lay on a gurney surrounded by other cadaver-laden trolleys in the basement of the medical examiner's office.

Charlie and Joe were sitting inside the air-conditioned office that overlooked the steel iceboxes filled with the bodies of other deceased persons.

Eddie Burke's body was not put away yet, as this was a hot issue that the detectives needed some answers on right away. Burke had been shot about four hours ago, according to the

Medical Examiner's preliminary examination, and he told them that he finally was able to reach the doctor that they were waiting on for the final answers to several important questions that the body should give up to them.

CHAPTER THIRTY-THREE

It was a few minutes later that a blond-haired young woman pushed her way into the air-conditioned room where the detectives were sitting. She appeared to be in her late thirties, dressed in tailored blue slacks and a white blouse, with a large medical bag in her left hand and a smile on her pretty face.

"Hi, guys. I'm Doctor Jackie Gibbons. I apologize for taking so long to get here. The Medical Examiner's office reached me just as I was leaving my office." Her professional eye roamed over the still forms just lying there on the gurneys.

Joe pointed out the cart that was holding Eddie. "I'm sorry, Doctor, but we haven't had the time to wash the body down yet. He is pretty much as we found him, as he was covered all over with dirt and gore. We thought it best if we left him just the way he was for you."

They all walked out of the room together.

"I'll need some water if I am going to perform the dental work you requested."

Charlie walked over to an attendant and asked for some water for the doctor's procedure.

She removed a chamois from her bag and spread it across the dead man's chest. She then took out a paper pad, two tubes that resembled toothpaste, a horseshoe-shaped instrument with a handle, a metal putty spatula, and three plastic cups.

The attendant came over with a liter of water in a plastic bottle. "How ya doing, Doc? Nice to see you" he said as he worked the bottle of water down between the cadaver's legs.

"Fine, thank you, Igor," she said.

When the attendant had gone, Charlie whispered at the doctor, "Igor?"

She smiled at him. "Yes, isn't that a pity."

She reached back into her bag again and came out with a rectangular block of hard rubber. She snapped on a pair of latex gloves, and pressed open the dead man's mouth. "Say ahhh," she muttered to herself, as she inserted the bite block between the back row of teeth in order to prop open the mouth.

She opened one of the tubes and squeezed out a two-inch strip of paste onto the pad. She did the same with the other tube and then using the spatula, she mixed the two strips into one large glob of sticky stuff.

Both detectives moved in closer to watch. This was a procedure that neither of them had seen before.

The doctor explained as she worked. "One of the compounds is a rubber based polyester impression material. The other compound is a catalyst. We stir them together until we get a homogeneous mix of fairly equal parts." She worked in silence for a minute or two with the spatula and waited until the paste mixture that was now in Eddie's mouth turned slightly purple.

"That should do it," she said as she picked up the horse-shoe shaped instrument. "This is an impression tray," she said as she removed the molds from Eddie's mouth and put the now-quick-dried impressions of the upper and lower teeth into the tray.

She mixed more paste, troweled it into one of the cups she had previously taken from her kit, and asked, "Who has the cigarettes?"

Joe removed the plastic evidence bag from his briefcase and handed it to her.

She removed one of the butts and held it up to the fluorescent light. Using both hands, she carefully smoothed the cigarette and implanted the filter from the cigarette into the paste. Turning her attention back to the cadaver, she took hold of the tray's handle and wiggled it free of the teeth. She removed the cast from the reservoir and put it down on the paper pad.

This done, she mixed more paste and repeated the procedure on the bottom row of teeth. After she had done that, she reached into Eddie's mouth and removed the bite block, wrapped it up in a disinfectant-soaked cloth, put it in a plastic bag and tossed it back into her open medical bag. She opened a jar of wax and picking up one of the molds, began layering wax around the outside of the impression.

"Why are you doing that?" Joe asked.

"In order to raise the base of the mold," she replied. "This way, I'll create a dam for the dental stone."

"Stone?"

"Dental stone is similar to plaster, only faster-drying," she said. "We mix it with water and pour the solution into the holes that the teeth made in the mold. When it dries we'll have a perfect replica of Eddie's teeth."

Joe looked down at the butt sticking up out of the cup. "Same procedure for that?"

"Yes," she said.

"How long will it be before you can tell us if Eddie smoked those cigarettes or was it someone else?"

"I can tell you that right now. Those impressions you wanted were not made by Eddie, the dead man. And there is no doubt about that."

The two detectives looked at each other. Another dead end.

CHAPTER THIRTY-FOUR

Detective Joe Wahl looked over at Charlie Glass with great admiration as he said, "I really can't believe you did that, Charlie. I didn't think you had the balls to do something like that."

Lead Detective Charlie Glass stared blankly at Joe and focused his eyes upon Sweetpea Soll, who was much more pleasant to look at.

The three Sheriff's Department employees were secure in their location at the Central Los Angeles County Jail where they had just left their former commander, Captain Crewe, under arrest in a protected holding cell underground in the sub-basement section of the huge facility.

The three of them had requested a private conference room for themselves away from everyone and everything. The private room would allow them the luxury of peace and quiet while they gathered themselves together. The three of them just sat there sipping at the coffee that Sweetpea had poured for them. They all shared in the comfort of each other's company and the solitude of the moment.

Based upon the major complaint sworn out by Detective Charles Glass, papers of arrest were issued against Sheriff's Captain Crewe and delivered to his home, where he was arrested by the Los Angeles Sheriff's In-House Enforcement Crew, who made the arrest in the early hours of that morning. The captain was up and dressed in his uniform and without a word being spoken to the arresting team, allowed them to read him his rights as he nodded at them that he completely understood everything.

The captain had taken a chance by telling Charlie everything that he did, and when Charlie left without talking to him it became obvious that there would soon be a knock on his door. The captain had no regrets that he had set things in motion with Charlie taking the lead. He realized that his time in the limelight that he was used to was all over.

He was ready and able to take any punishment that would be given to him in the future, but for right now he knew that the information that he had in his head as to names, locations and other vital information would allow him to make a deal for himself. Right now he just wanted punishment and justice to be done to make up for the mistakes he had allowed to go on under his protection. He was very much ashamed of himself as he looked back at the things he had allowed to happen under his watch.

While the captain was cooling his heels in the Sheriff's secure holding cell, Charlie, Joe and Sweetpea were all carefully listening to the speaker telephone that had Inspector Roberto Sanchez reading to them from some papers found in the captain's home. When the captain was arrested, the team that took him into custody also legally served him with a search warrant that allowed them to go through his home and look for anything that seemed to be of interest to the case. He was asked for, and without any difficulty of any kind, gave them the combination to the holding safe and security cabinet located in his master bedroom.

Inspector Sanchez was reading aloud to the three of them from several papers that he thought might be important to their case. The Inspector said that he would bring everything in to the Sheriff's office later in the day and have copies made for them, but he thought a few things that attracted his attention should be read to them posthaste. The inspector was reading very slowly and clearly as Sweetpea, who was an expert in shorthand note-taking, was taking things down word for word. The three of them would go over her transcript after the Inspector signed off.

Very shortly Inspector Sanchez said goodbye, and that they could pick up transcripts of what he read to them at headquarters after ten tomorrow morning.

After the call was disconnected, Charlie asked Sweetpea if she would get them all some fresh coffee, and take an extra hour doing so. He said that he needed to talk privately with his Number Two Investigator about some things that she was not cleared to listen to. He also asked her to leave her notes on the table.

With a nod of understanding on her face, Sweetpea smiled at them both and left the secure room. She had been in the Sheriff's Legal Department for many years, and she knew how these things worked. She thought to herself that besides getting the coffee and some nibble-food for them all, she would make a stop at the ladies' room while she had the opportunity.

When the door closed behind Sweetpea, Charlie asked Joe if he would take over the discussion, and throw in his thoughts and observations that he had been keeping to himself for the past eighteen years since he first saw the double murders on Mulholland Drive. Charlie watched quietly as Joe Wahl spread out Sweetpea's notes on the table in front of him.

Joe read them over once and then re-read them again. He tilted his chair backward, looked up at the ceiling and began to speak.

"Charlie, what I am going to say to you now is off the record, and will be denied by me as having ever said this to you if we ever go to court on this.

Ever since I caught the case as a rookie cop over eighteen years ago, I knew that there was something wrong with the way the Mulholland Drive double-murder investigation was being handled. Whatever little evidence we were able to put together was never entered on the books, and things disappeared from the evidence lockers whenever I went back inside to look for them. I knew that I was standing alone just whistling into a strong headwind, so I shut my mouth, did the everyday job the way I was supposed to do it, and waited.

What was I waiting for? I was waiting for you, Charlie. I was waiting for some other dumb cop who could not be bought, and who would not look the other way when told to do so. I was waiting for you, and here you are, my own personal number one. You are a breath of fresh air to a drowning man, Charlie Glass, and here is what I think has been going on for a long, long time inside the Sheriff's Department.

The double shooting eighteen years ago was an obvious discipline lesson for everyone involved to take orders and stay in line. It was too professional to be just a lover's-lane kind of killing, and it had all the earmarks of a professional hit. The only professional hit men who could pull this off at that time were in Cosa Nostra, or the Mob.

Right after Mulholland, we saw the Mob moving into the local businesses, and we were told, in clear and precise words from higher-ups, that since no one was getting hurt, look the other way. There were two or three cops who just would not do so, and they were either forced out of the department or made to retire before their pensions were pulled away from them.

I learned quickly to always keep my mouth shut, and as a result the bad things always seemed to pass me by. I knew someone with the rank of captain or higher was keeping things calm, but I never could figure out who.

Billions and billions of dollars were being made at the downtown Los Angeles alley stores. As a result of this success, other businesses were falling in line, and since no one ever got hurt, there were no charges ever brought, and therefore I had nowhere to go with my thoughts and suspicions, so I just kept my mouth shut and went through the motions of being a good cop.

Now you are here, Charlie, and you listened to me when I told you about the Mulholland Drive killings being done by the same perp, and you listened and remembered. When I mentioned things to you that I could not tell anyone else, nothing ever came back to hit me in the face. You, Charlie, were for real. So quietly I began to trace the movement of men and evidence from the other case back to Captain Crewe's desk.

I did not say anything to anyone because I knew that he had to have someone higher up in our department that he reported to. The captain was able to head off problems before they ever got out of hand, and he could only do so with the help of someone higher up at city hall.

I never was able to put it together that it was Councilman Ganz who was the inside man until he was killed. It had to be the boys from the Mob who made the hit that killed him. I ruled out just about anyone else from city hall being involved. Sweetpea's notes from the captain named the other two councilmen who were killed at that city hall raid. And there was one other clerk who had to have been on their payroll, because he was able to give days and dates when all three of them would be in the building.

The captain took his marching orders from the councilmen, and I believe that he actually limited himself to as little insider information as he could. That, of course, makes Captain Crewe of no use to us at this time.

But what I think can be useful is to go back to the captain's bank deposits and see where checks came from that went into and out of his account. I would bet my next month's salary that the bank he used was the Bank of Italy, which conveniently is located throughout our own state of California.

And why do I say that one specific bank, you might ask? I would make my educated guess based on the background of the founders of the bank, who always have bragged about their coming to America from Italy as poorly funded working-class men.

Suddenly, these working-class men were opening up branches all up and down the state of California, with the majority centered right here in Los Angeles.

Is it an accident the Cosa Nostra Mob was always pure Italian? We all know that one had to be Italian to get into the Mob in the first place. And you had to be Italian to work your way up the Mob ladder of success.

If you think about it, it was a perfect place for the drug, prostitution and money-lending activities that were generated to be cleanly washed of any hint of bad things and end up as conservation bank loans to the unsuspecting public.

I could be wrong, but all the evidence points one way, and that way is the way of the Mob.

CHAPTER THIRTY-FIVE

The hour was up, and we find Sweetpea back in the secure room with Charlie and Joe. She had brought a fresh pot of coffee and a lot of cookies and nibble-food with her. She finally settled into her chair at the table and looked expectantly at the two men who sat there completely at peace with each other. Sweetpea recognized that her two guys had come to an agreement on the case and whatever else was needed and necessary in order to go forward.

Charlie picked up the lead once again and asked Sweetpea to type up the notes that she had taken and put them into the open file on the Mulholland Drive case. In much fewer words than Joe would have used, he brought her up to the moment on all the points that were discussed by them on the case and the organized crime involvement.

Charlie signed a paper he had just written to the head of the legal department where Sweetpea was assigned, requesting that she be released from all other duties that she was doing for the legal department so that she could give all her efforts to this fast-breaking case. Sweetpea would be the only connection between Charlie's investigating unit and the Legal Department from the Sheriff's Department.

He requested that all information be sealed and could only be opened with two of the following three signatures. He listed Sandra (Sweetpea) Soll, Detective Joseph Wahl, and himself, Detective

Charles Glass. If anything happened to one or more of the three signers, a new signature person could be added by the Sheriff or the Under-Sheriff only. There was to be no other authorized access to the file.

After a few more minutes of conversation between the three of them, they all separated to get things rolling. Sweetpea was going up to the Legal Department to file the papers Charlie has just given to her. She would set up the files and open up several secure lines that would be working only between the three of them at all times. Joe was dispatched to follow up on anything that seemed important from the information given up to them from the captain's papers. Charlie told them both that he was going to take himself for a quiet drive to clear his head and see if he could put together a plan of action for them to get started with. They would meet up at a later time.

§

I took out one of the unmarked police cars and started working my way in light traffic toward Century City. In the notes that Sweetpea had written down from the Inspector who went into Captain Crewe's private papers was the name da Vinci Enterprises, at the address that I was now headed for. I wanted to get a look at the public face of what I was now sure was La Costa Nostra, or as it was called on the streets of L.A., the Organization.

It was a cloudy afternoon and the sun was trying to break through the clouds as I turned my car off of Santa Monica Boulevard and onto Century Park East. I followed the slow traffic as it passed famous streets named Galaxy Way, Avenue Of The Stars, and Constellation Boulevard. As usual, I realized that Los Angeles is very famous for its self-adornments.

I was approaching my destination, which was the Century Plaza Towers, a matched set of square buildings that stand thirty-five stories high. I knew for a fact that the towers were full of agents and lawyers for the movie industry, and as I pulled into the valet parking lot, I was looking at dozens of Porsches, Jags, and shiny Mercedes just waiting for their owners to come bounding out of the building.

The Century Plaza Towers are the biggest buildings in Century City. They have to be, in order to squeeze in the egos of all their tenants.

I stood in front of the buildings' directory as I looked up the location of my destination. There it was, da Vinci Enterprises, LLC, located in the Western Towers Penthouse.

When I stepped out of the elevator and into a beautifully designed waiting room, I saw enormous glass windows that completely enclosed the room. I could see a three-hundred-sixty-degree view of the greater Los Angeles area. In spite of myself, I was greatly impressed.

The clear glass room was tastefully hung with reproductions of dozens of paintings by Leonardo da Vinci. They ran from miniatures of the Last Supper all the way to an excellent print of the Mona Lisa. I realized that with the famous name of da Vinci on the door that these pictures and prints were in good taste. I thought that they must have cost a fortune.

A beautiful Asian lady sat behind the chrome and glass desk that dominated the room. She was wearing a headphone that curved downward to a small microphone that was perched on the side of her mouth. I gave her my best smile and introduced myself as Detective Charlie Glass of the Los Angeles Sheriff's Department. I asked her if I could speak with Mr. da Vinci upon a very important matter. She murmured something into her microphone and told me that someone would come out for me shortly.

It was only a minute or two until I looked up from where I was sitting when my name was called. An absolutely stunning young woman was standing in the open doorway smiling wonderfully at me. She was tall, very trim, well-built, and quite elegant. "Please follow me, Detective Glass. Mr. da Vinci is waiting for you."

She led me back along a block of quiet corridors, through an amazingly designed glass door, and into an outer office that has probably been set up for the executive secretary to Mr. da Vinci. We stopped at double doors that appear to have the coat of arms of the da Vinci family on them.

"Please go right in," she said.

The man behind the desk looked at my business card for a little while without picking it up, and then, finally, he looked up at me and smiled.

It was a great smile and I could tell that he knew it was. The small lines around his eyes made him look both kind and wise at the same time. The firm indentations around his mouth gave him a look of sincerity. The overall impression that I had from him was that here was a man who liked to be in control.

With that special smile on his face, he stood up from behind his desk, walked around it and extended his hand for mine. He stood quite close to me as we shook hands, which allowed him to tower over me. To my credit, I think, I did not step back.

The man was a walking advertisement right out of the latest issue of *Gentlemen's Quarterly*. His eyes, which were emerald green beneath a square-cut reddish-bronze mane of hair, were recording my every move. His face was deeply tanned with freckles here and there. He had several deep scars on his face that varied from light to deep. They simply added depth to his already-impressive character.

Here was a very muscular, broad-shouldered man, who stands well over six foot two and is probably a slim two-hundred pounder. His walk was as graceful and smooth as a large jungle cat, and I had the distinct feeling that he was a man whose basic instincts were quite primitive, but that, to his personal credit, he successfully covered that primitive self with highly civilized manners. I am very impressed with this Mr. da Vinci.

We finally seated ourselves and, after the usual chitchat made between two males when first they meet, got down to business.

I decided to try a direct approach because beating around the bush with this sophicated kind of guy would be a gigantic waste of time. "As you can see by the card you are holding in your hand, Mr. da Vinci, I am a Detective for the Los Angeles Sheriff's Department, and your name has come up in connection to a case that I am working on"

Mr. da Vinci looks once again at my business card and puts it carefully into his jacket pocket. "I see, Detective Glass, that you are assigned to the Sheriff's Central Division, which I believe is downtown. I have a friend who also works there. Perhaps you know him. His name is Captain Crewe."

"I do know him quite well, Mr. da Vinci, and as a matter of fact, it is because of Captain Crewe that I wanted to meet you in person. I seem to have heard some interesting things about you, and I thought I would introduce myself. And now that I know you, and you know me, I would like to thank you for your time." With a smile on his face, Detective Charlie Glass stood up and walked to the beautifully engraved glass door and let himself out of the office and walked slowly down the hallway that he had used to make his entrance.

In his mind's eye, Charlie pictured Mr. da Vinci on the telephone as he reached out to see if Captain Crewe could explain to him why a visitation was made to his office by one of his detectives. A little line of worry might cross the handsome brow of Mr. da Vinci when he found out that he could not get a return call from the captain.

Charlie was a happy man. He just loved stirring up the pot to see what would happen.

CHAPTER THIRTY-SIX

Lead Detective Charlie Glass, for the very first time since he was assigned the Mulholland Drive Double Murder Case, was beginning to feel good about the turn of events that the case was suddenly taking on.

Organized crime had been identified as the bad guys, and their controller for the Los Angeles area was given a positive identification by Captain Crewe and confirmed by himself as the da Vinci person that he had met in Century City.

He had Detective Joe Wahl on backup with his special knowledge and his dedication to this very same case for the past eighteen years. His accumulated insights were in-valuable and his anger and frustration for all those years made him a great asset.

He had Sweetpea as his legal contact to the court system for any legal actions and papers that would be needed. Sweetpea had herself assigned to the case on a full-time basis as of this morning. Sweetpea was wonderfully organized and would be putting all the papers and notes into proper form so that if and when they needed a judge to approve a court order for arrests, the paperwork would be at their fingertips.

He also just picked up and had Field Inspector Roberto Sanchez assigned to his growing team of specialists. Field Inspector Sanchez would lead the muscle from the Sheriff's office when it was needed in the rounding-up of the bad guys. They would do any and all arrests that were to be made All that Charlie had to do was figure out who was who.

And figuring out what piece of the puzzle went where was the reason that Charlie asked that all members of his new crew meet him in the large meeting room just outside the captain's holding cell early that morning.

When everyone was assembled and introductions to Inspector Sanchez were completed, Charlie asked that the captain be brought in to join them. Charlie had sent in a note earlier to the captain telling him who would be at the meeting and what information they were looking for from him. Since the captain knew everyone already, and had hired most of them, the meeting could either be a pleasant one or one that was under great pressure.

§

A smiling and relaxed Captain Crewe put everyone at ease. He made the rounds, shaking the hand of everyone in the room except for Sweetpea, to whom he gave the usual kiss on the cheek.

It was obvious that the captain had taken a great load off his shoulders when he confessed to Charlie in the roundabout manner that he did about his connection to what was going on. The violence that was so unexpected had caused the captain to change sides, and it was hoped that inside his head there would be enough information for them to proceed at full speed. But this was not to be so.

The captain was very cooperative, but he did not really know much about everything that was going on in the city. His information was limited to the da Vinci guy and his City Council handlers, who would give the captain his instructions when something was needed by the Mob. Beyond this tip of the iceberg, the captain was out of his element and left the meeting with a brave smile on his face but a sadness in his heart for all the damage he had allowed.

Charlie listened to everyone's thoughts, but nothing came up that was new or different, and so he dismissed them all except for Joe, his second-in-command. The two of them left together and walked slowly down Grand Avenue and away from the Sheriff's buildings. Once again, nothing much that was new popped up. Charlie called it a day, and they went their separate ways.

CHAPTER THIRTY-SEVEN

Nothing much was happening on the case as Charlie and Joe were sipping coffee again at the local coffee shop around the comer from headquarters the next morning.

Joe was trying to make a point about how useless facts and statistics were if you looked at them all by themselves. He was saying that based upon all on his years of experience with the Sheriff's Department, the odds of something special occurring that will give you a heads-up usually doesn't happen. Things are never that easy.

He went on to say that odds on something are just mathematical projections that a particular event will or won't occur. He explained that if the odds of a plane crash are one to one million against it happening, then the chance of there being a plane crash is extremely low. This might sound silly, because of our being familiar with odds on gambling, but that is the correct mathematical expression.

On the other hand, when your odds of dying from the bite of a snake in the jungle are ninety-nine in one hundred chances, wear your heavy boots or just stay out of the jungle.

When there is a certainty that something won't happen, it's expressed as "zero probability." If there is a fifty-fifty chance, then we call that "even odds." At the opposite side of this probability projection is that something absolutely certain will happen. This is expressed as one hundred percent, since there is no chance that something specific won't happen.

He believed that, based on the odds of probability he just explained, that at least one, and possibly two, of the City Hall shooters woud be found just as dead as the first shooter, identified as Eddie, and he or they will have met a violent death.

Charlie just smiled at his number two and continued to sip at his coffee.

§

As it turned out only four days later, Detective Joe Wahl was absolutely correct.

One of the remaining shooters who were still out there was out there no more. His body was found in an alley somewhere on the East Side of Los Angeles. That left only one known suspect from the City Hall shooting unaccounted for, and Charlie wanted him found alive.

He immediately kicked the entire Sheriff's Department's search sequence program into action and sent out a picture of the last known shooter to every officer, hotel, motel, rental location in the greater Los Angeles area. The hope was that someone would see the picture and contact the Sheriff's Department with information on his whereabouts. And then they got lucky.

Within forty-eight hours, the suspect was located in nearby Ventura County, and was properly identified as the suspect and held for pick-up by the Los Angeles Sheriff's Department. He was taken to the Central Men's Jail, where he was put into solitary confinement so that no one within or outside the department could get to him.

The four names on the authorized list for access to the prisoner were Sweetpea, Joe, Roberto, and Charlie. The four of them were gathered at this moment in the large office next to the secure holding cell where the suspect was being held. Fingerprints had determined that the shooter was a citizen of Italy by the name of Vinnie Votello. He was here on a temporary visa as a bidder for supplies for a City Hall project of some sort or other.

Inspector Roberto Sanchez was speaking: "All professional gunmen are faced with two distinctly different kinds of killings. The first is in 'hot blood,' which is an instant heat that is usually generated by a particular situation, usually in defense of their own life or their employer's. The second kind of killing is a completely different proposition altogether, and this is what we are looking at right now. This is a cold and calculating business situation where the situation is carefully assessed, and the risks are all worked out in advance of the actual killing. But often, even that is not enough. The mental preparation is just as important. It is the winding up of the killer's whole personality like a clock spring, so that when the moment does actually arrive, there is an instant readiness to kill.

"In the final analysis, this is what sets apart the real professional killer from the rest of the field. A willingness to kill a stranger without the slightest hesitation is something that most people never hope to do, and that is why high-level shooters like our Vinnie in there are in high demand for their services. Usually a shooter like Vinnie completes his contract, gets paid, and simply disappears back to where he or she came from.

"In this case, something happened. We don't know why it happened, but one of their shooters was killed from within their own organization, and the other killers, knowing that their lives were in danger, tried their best to completely disappear. However, they were unable to get out of town on their own, due to the fast reaction time of this team's leader, Charlie Glass, who shut them out of the usual escape routes. Obviously, the remaining shooters went under cover, and it was only Vinnie who survived long enough for us to find and grab him and then secure his whereabouts.

"And here is the interesting answer to your inquiry to my office earlier, Charlie, about the answering machine at Captain Crew's old location. We have a record of three calls coming in from the da Vinci offices in Century City where you made your visits. You made quite an impression to get such a fast response from this da Vinci character!

"It was quite obvious due to the urgency in Mr. da Vinci's voice that he wanted to speak to the captain "posthaste." But with the good captain in residence here at our secure location, there was no conversation between the two of them. Automatically a tap was put onto all the da Vinci telephones at his home as well as at the office. As of this moment, I have nothing of interest to report from either telephone."

Sweetpea Soll followed the Inspector with her detailed report that all information upon organized crime within the city limits of Los Angeles, beginning immediately, would be routed to her desk for review. So far, she said, there was nothing of any interest to report, but she would be watching all incoming calls, voice and e-mails. She was also preparing all the paperwork needed for their special task force in case they had a need to serve any legal papers on anyone in the area that could provide them with anything out of the ordinary. She finished up be saying that she had a direct telephone line into her supervisor's office at the Legal Department in case they needed a search warrant or any other legal document on short notice.

Then Joe Wahl took the floor and expressed his feelings of pleasure at getting some answers to several of his old cases, and for their bringing into the open for the first time the underground movements that had been going on in the Mob for many, many years. He did caution that each of them had to keep an eye out for anything that seemed out of the ordinary. He suggested to Charlie, who immediately nodded his acknowledgement of an excellent idea, that each of them be given a personal bodyguard/ driver so that they could all avoid any unfortunate "accidents" that might pop up in their daily schedule without a "driver."

Charlie added that he would see to it that they all had twenty-four-hour security around them at all times until this case was closed.

Charlie waited until Joe had finished up and asked if there was anything else that anyone wanted to bring up before he took his turn. He took the floor and smiled deeply at each and every one of his new partners. Hopefully they could do some great things together. The potential was there and each of them knew the door of opportunity would be open to them if and when the team did something extraordinary.

CHAPTER THIRTY-EIGHT

"Before any of us talk directly to Vinnie, who has been kind enough to visit us next door in the holding tank, I wanted to fill us all in on the information that I requested from the FBI. I have a copy of what they sent over for everyone, and I wanted to go over the few pages so that it would help us understand the thinking of our prize prisoner.

"I thought for the first interview that Joe and Roberto would be the most effective. Sweetpea and I will be watching through the two-way glass mirror located on the back wall of the holding room. Your conversation with Vinnie will be recorded and as soon as Sweetpea has the time, she will make copies for each of us. I am hoping that Vinnie knows some names and organization information that he can trade with us for a lighter sentence from the judge for his cooperation.

"I have here a short copy for each of us from the Feds on information on the Mob in Los Angeles. I found it interesting and I think we should all flip through it before we officially meet Vincent the shooter."

§

FOR THE EYES ONLY OF DETECTIVE CHARLIE GLASS'S COMMITTEE OF FOUR – FROM THE FBI FILES ON

ORGANIZED CRIME LIMITED TO THE GREATER LOS ANGELES, CALIFORNIA, AREA

Italian Mafia: also called Cosa Nostra, Camorra, 'Ndanghata and Sacra Corona Unita

This Italian organized-crime group has long been dominated by a multitude of clans and mob families, all generally referred to as the "Mafia." The term "Mafia" broadly implies that these gangs, besides running a series of illicit businesses, all pervade local society environments in which they operate, and influence many aspects of public and private lives in order to cement their powers. The Sicilian Mafia, AKA Cosa Nostra, is the oldest of the five (5) Italian crime syndicates. The term "Mafia" was used exclusively to indicate what would later become known simply as "Cosa Nostra."

Cosa Nostra reached its power peak in the Los Angeles area a few years ago, around the year 1980.

The Mafia in Los Angeles is mainly involved in local criminal activities such as infiltrating public construction works and running extortion rackets. According to our own FBI sources, the Mob holds the most successful high political business roles in the city. More than any other crime syndicate, Cosa Nostra has historically expanded from the criminal world into the more traditional and quieter world of normal trade and business practices.

Part of the Mob's success is due to its very secretive nature. As clans are formed on strict blood ties, members rarely turn informers, and this makes detective work and law enforcement much more difficult. They do not cooperate with authorities because it would mean turning in a relative or a close family member. Such a close structure allows the mob to create a stable presence among all of its members.

Besides the drug traffic trade, these gangs are involved in

pretty much any profitable illicit activity, except for prostitution. For some reason we do not know, they stay away from it.

Los Angeles mobsters have a tendency to show off their riches that have been amassed through crime. The average mobsters usually come from working-class poor families and are inclined to boast about their sudden enrichment.

Summary

The two most powerful Mob cities have always been New York and Chicago. The Los Angeles mob was actually quite notorious, but it was considered to be somewhat inept compared to the other Mafia families. To this moment, the two most powerful families work out of New York and Chicago. The Chicago Mafia, which calls itself "the outfit," controls the half of the country west of the Mississippi River. Las Vegas is considered to be a special case, and it was divided up initially between New York and Chicago, holding each in its sway.

CHAPTER THIRTY-NINE

The rap sheet on the shooter Vinnie Votello, who was patiently waiting his for his interview, was a short one. He was a citizen of Milan, Italy, whose passport information said that he was in Los Angeles on a business trip for purchases of building materials for his company.

The Sheriff's paperwork said that he understood and spoke English, but spoke with a heavy accent. He was five foot seven inches tall and weighed in at one hundred and ninety-three pounds. He was thirty-four years old and this was his third trip to the United States. There was nothing in the paperwork saying that he was a professional shooter or anything else but a businessman.

He told his interviewers that, along with his two companion shooters, he had visited the Los Angles City Hall two times before the day of the shooting. This was to allow them to get familiar with where they would be going on the day they would turn into the killers that they were hired to be. When Vinnie was promised a better deal for the jail time that everyone knew he would be facing, he agreed to tell the authorities everything he knew.

As it turned out, he could give exact detailed accounts of the meetings that they all had with the person who was known as "the handler," but not much else. The handler went by the first name of Pietro, and he spoke English and Italian perfectly. It was Pietro who provided them with female companions while they spent the few days waiting for their contracts to begin. Vinnie said that up to the actual day of the shooting; that things were moving along quite properly. All food and wine were provided for them, but they were not allowed to leave the hotel room, which was located somewhere on the East Side of downtown Los Angeles.

Vinnie said that he heard the end of one conversation between Pietro and the person that he took his orders from, whom he called Mr. D. It was assumed but not proven that Mr. D would turn out to be the same Mr. da Vinci that Charlie had introduced himself to.

The interview with Vinnie ended with a lot of general knowledge of the inner working of the so-called "hit squad," but nothing else of interest was taken away from the meeting. A disappointed but not completely unhappy Charlie Glass watched as the last of the shooters was re-escorted by a Sheriff's Deputy back to his holding cell.

The legal process would catch up with Vinnie in the next few days. Charlie would live up to his given word and request that the court give Vinnie some sort of lesser sentence because of the various bits and pieces of information that they were able to pull out of him regarding his relationship with the Cosa Nostra both here in the United States and back in Italy.

It was still not clear to any of the interviewers, nor to Vinnie himself, as to why the Organization had turned their backs on the three shooters, who, by all of the leading indicators, had completed their contracts as ordered. Only time would tell about that, but in the meantime the Sheriff's Department had established some insider information about the da Vinci person, and where and how illegal money from the 'boys', found its way to the streets of Central Los Angeles via the Alley merchants who were working in downtown Los Angeles.

Charlie asked Sweetpea to do a complete search of the official records on the recent double homicide on Mulholland Drive. He wanted to know immediately who it was that was watching his number two, Joe Wahl, for the Department, when Charlie was having some doubts about him. Even though it was Charlie who had authorized the twenty-four-hour watch upon Joe, he never knew who it was that was keeping a very professional eye on him. Not a glimmer and not a glance of anyone ever showed up, and yet someone was watching Joe Wahl, because his minute-by-minute movements around town were recorded and entered into the Mulholland file in great detail.

Charlie had never learned who it was that put such a great watchful eye on Joe, and now that he was the lead investigator on the case, he could request that information and have that person sent into his office for a face-to-face meeting. Charlie wanted to grab onto this person for his own team. Anyone that neither he nor Joe Wahl could identify must be some sort of invisible man, and he wanted this invisible man to be on the assignment of watching the da Vinci guy from the inner city. Charlie had no idea of who it was until the observers of Joe Wahl, super detective, walked into his office, and they both sat down on the chairs facing Charlie.

Now, Charlie was a great movie fan and he never would miss a Laurel and Hardy movie whenever the reruns were shown at one of the local movie houses or at home on the television screen. Laurel and Hardy were a comedy double act during the early classical Hollywood era of American cinema. The team was composed of the Englishman Stan Laurel (1890–1963) and heavyset American Oliver Hardy (1892–1957). They became well known during the late 1920s thought the early 1940s for their slapstick comedy, with Laurel playing the clumsy and childlike friend of the pompous Hardy. They appeared as a team in 107 films, starring in three short silent films, 40 short sound films and 23 full-length feature films.

And now, sitting in his office right in front of him, wearing shiny Sheriff's badges on their shirts, were Arnie Archibald and Bobby Licht. Arnie & Bobby reminded Charlie very much of

Laurel & Hardy.

It was immediately obvious to Charlie that he had seen both men around the office and even sometimes out in the field. Neither one of the two faces would stand out in a crowd, and that was just what Charlie was looking for. Two everyday faces who did not stand out in a crowd! They were just what the doctor ordered to watch Century City's da Vinci and friends.

Arnie Archibald and Bobby Licht smiled at Charlie as they opened up the standard information package that they received. Charlie watched as each man read through the briefing papers, laughed out loud a few times, smiled at him and left the room.

Charlie, who was holding the original copy of the papers, was going to take a few minutes to read for a second time the folder on Mr. da Vinci of Century City. He knew why the two investigators had laughed when they read his briefing papers, and Charlie smiled to himself as he opened up the file to look at everything for the second time. It wasn't very often that something like this brought a smile to the face of whoever read the file.

CHAPTER FORTY

Charlie opened up the assignment book and put his full attention upon the briefing papers that he had given to the two undercover agents who were going to be watching da Vinci on a day to day basis. One of the computer experts at the Sheriff's Central Office had put together the information upon receiving Charlie's written request. It read as follows:

FOR THE EYES ONLY OF UNDERCOVER AGENTS ARNIE ARCHIBALD AND BOBBY LICHT AS ORDERED BY LEAD DETECTIVE CHARLES GLASS.

The person to be watched is L. da Vinci, who works out of the Twin Towers area in Century City, California. L. da Vinci is a suspect in the double murders on Mulholland Drive and the recent shooting at Los Angeles City Hall. The initial that Mr. da Vinci uses is the letter L, and he says that it stands for his first name of Leonardo.

This Mr. Leonardo da Vinci claims that he is the eighteenth family member to use the full name of Leonardo da Vinci and that he is a direct descendant of the famous man. This Leonardo da

Vinci signs his documents as Leonardo da Vinci XVIII.

Mr. da Vinci XVIII claims his fame goes back to the famous picture of the *Mona Lisa* that was painted by the original artist in the 1400s.

§

Here is the story as relayed by the computer on the connection between Leonardo da Vinci and the *Mona Lisa* picture that he is known to have painted:

On August 21, 1911, a small-time French portrait painter was setting up his artist's easel in the Salon Carré, a room in one of the most famous museums of Paris, France, the Louvre. There are well over twenty very small side rooms in the Louvre that directly face the location where the portrait of the *Mona Lisa* smiles out at her admirers.

Louis Beroud, the painter, was planning to paint his copy of the *Mona Lisa* portrait as he had done many times before, but this time something was very wrong. There was a completely empty space where the picture should have been hanging.

When he first asked the guard who was walking around where the *Mona Lisa* was supposed to be, he was told that it probably was in the photography room where copies of portraits were made. Louis Beroud waited patiently for the painting's return, but finally he was getting very impatient, so he asked the guard once again about where the *Mona Lisa* portrait was, and why it was taking so long just to have a photograph made.

The guard checked with his supervisor and then went back to Louis Beroud. The artist was now pacing back and forth in front of the empty space where the *Mona Lisa* should have been. The guard, with a definite shake in his voice, admitted that the portrait was … gone.

It seems that the most famous painting in today's world was not very well known at the turn of the twentieth century. The painting was only appreciated by art professionals and a very few others. The general public was completely unaware of it.

But the news of the theft caught the public's imagination, and it transformed the simple painting into a cultural icon. The whole civilized world was suddenly talking about it, not only the local French. Suddenly, the whereabouts of the *Mona Lisa* became a red-hot item! The picture's likeness began to show up on posters, postcards, coffee mugs, in nightclubs, on movie screens, and anywhere else that was imaginable. Perhaps the strangest part of this whole story was the fact that record crowds of people from around the world began to show up at the museum just to look at the empty space where the painting used to hang. The burning question of the moment was, where was the *Mona Lisa*?

All kinds of theories were being talked about in France. With the first World War just getting ready to start, many people thought that the Germans, who were the number-one enemy of France at that time, had taken it in order to humiliate the French. Others thought that it was probably an elaborate practical joke that was intended to stir up interest in the museum.

It took well over ten days before the detailed search of the entire museum was completed. They never found the portrait, but what did turn up was the painting's empty frame. They located it at the very top of a tall staircase in the rear of the museum. It was believed that this location was probably the final escape route taken by the thief.

The months passed by quickly, and for two years there was no sign of the painting. The fascinating question at that time was what would an art thief have done with the portrait? At that time it was valued at five million dollars, and today, as we all know, it is priceless.

To whom could the thief sell the painting? Even if a buyer could be found and was willing to spend that much money, wasn't the painting too high-profile to be passed easily along the art-thief network? It would have been too easy to trace! The crook would have been caught without difficulty no matter where in the world he tried to sell it.

The answer finally came on November 29, 1913. A very wealthy art dealer, Alfred Gert, had a note passed to him one evening at a dinner party that he was attending. The note was from someone whom he did not know. The note, from a person who called himself Leonardo Vincenzo, offered to return the *Mona Lisa* portrait to him for a fee.

Alfred Gert thought that it was a hoax, another practical joke of many that were going around. He was intrigued enough, however, to put together a meeting at a local Florence hotel. He invited the museum's chief of staff and the local police to attend the meeting with him.

The two men walked into the hotel room, and the police waited patiently outside and out of sight. Once inside the room, they encountered a short, mustachioed Italian man who told them that he left Italy and moved to Paris at the time of the famous art theft. He then reached underneath the unmade bed and pulled out a long object that was very carefully wrapped in red silk.

The museum director, who was an art expert, unrolled the covering and examined the painting in great detail. His examination was very careful and very complete. He declared that the painting in front of him was authentic. It was the real *Mona Lisa* portrait.

The bottom line, or the end of this story, was that Leonardo Vincenzo, the thief, did not receive his ransom money. Instead he was arrested right on the spot and taken to the local police station, where he freely admitted that he was the one who stole the *Mona Lisa.*

On the morning of the theft, he explained, he entered the museum dressed in a flowing painter's smock. He went straight for the *Mona Lisa* painting, and he recalled that there were no other visitors or guards anywhere in sight. He removed the painting from the four wall hooks, hid it under his loose-fitting smock, frame and all, and then he simply walked out of the exhibit hall. When he reached the rear staircase, he removed the painting from the frame and continued on his way. The entire theft took about twenty minutes from start to finish.

So why did he do it? Why did he take the *Mona Lisa*?

He said it was for "love of my country, which is Italy." He said this clearly and loudly when he had his day in the French courts. He said that the *Mona Lisa* belonged in Italy, not France. He said that when Italy's greatest artist, Leonardo da Vinci, painted the portrait, Leonardo's intention was to leave the picture within the country of his origin, which, of course, was Italy. The little thief made a very interesting defense for himself, and the French press took hold of it and ran many days' worth of headlines with it.

The French judge who was hearing the case later remarked to the press that he had seriously thought of letting the little thief go, but his past criminal record of burglaries along with other various offenses convinced him that Leonardo Vincenzo's motivation was "less than patriotic." The judge sentenced him to seven months in jail. And when Vincenzo died in 1927, he was still bragging about being one of Italy's greatest patriots. The people of Italy were not really sure if he was a hero or just a confidence man, and mostly they left him alone.

As for the now-famous picture of *Mona Lisa,* it had made a triumphant return to the museum in France, where today the *Mona Lisa* smiles out from her impregnable climate-controlled bulletproof case. The picture averages about five million admirers each year with tourists and locals who come to the museum simply to see her famous smile.

Charlie closed the folder, and placed it carefully into the locked safe, shut off the lights and headed home for a good night's sleep.

CHAPTER FORTY-ONE

Daily reports started coming in to Charlie from his new two field men.

They described da Vinci as tall, solidly built, with not an ounce of fat evident anywhere. He seemed to have superhuman energy and endurance. He was handsome and charismatic with reddish-bronze hair and green eyes, and he carried himself with the absolute elegance of a natural athlete.

da Vinci's father, who also claimed a direct lineage to the original Leonardo da Vinci, proved himself to be a drunkard, and only after his only son moved away did the youngster free himself from the bad days of his childhood. By his mid-thirties, he had great success in the pharmacy line and also as a part-timer in the merchant marine. He moved early in his life into the wealthy community of Malibu, which is an exclusive housing development on the oceanfront in Southern California.

He appeared to the observers to be abrupt, impatient, and easily angered by anything not to his liking. He seemed to be a very difficult man to get along with, and all his known associates appeared to be business-related and never personal. He had a fatal tendency to make fun of and ridicule those with whom he disagreed. He can be summarized as brilliant, outspoken and quite antagonizing to even his closest friends and associates.

He is not married and has no former wives or children that can be located.

END REPORT

§

Charlie read the report and filed it into the safe where he kept everything related to the Mulholland Drive murder files and notes. He was completely satisfied with his observers and sent them notification that they were to stay on da Vinci until he pulled them off. He wanted to know who da Vinci saw and where he saw them, and asked for the observer's conclusions of anything and everything that was going on around da Vinci.

He made a few telephone calls, touched base with Sweetpea and left his office.

Things were slowly falling into place. He believed that da Vinci was one of the main keys to the Mob, and he was keeping him and all his known associates under close watch.

Joe Wahl was wandering around the Santee Alley stores and was busy playing tourist. Hopefully, he would be able to buy a few illegal/hot items so that they could put some big-time pressure on the vendors to tell them what was really happening on the streets of downtown Los Angeles.

CHAPTER FORTY-TWO

Sipping slowly at his morning coffee, Detective Second Grade Charlie Glass opened up the latest report from the undercover agents working on the da Vinci investigation.

§

FOR THE EYES ONLY OF LEAD DETECTIVE
CHARLES GLASS – SHERIFF'S DEPARTMENT
– LOS ANGELES, CALIFORNIA

As requested, we have done an in-depth investigation of the headquarters of the suspect known as Leonardo da Vinci and must report our failure in not being able to enter into the location of the above-mentioned suspect's place of business, located within one of the Century Towers buildings in Century City, California.

In order for us to get into the building we would need detailed security clearance and the getting of this clearance would announce our investigation to the suspect. Therefore it must be understood that we are only able to follow and document the whereabouts of the subject whenever he leaves the building.

It is our understanding that da Vinci enterprises is a tenant occupying the top floor of one of the towers and a basement meeting room which our sources tell us can not be spied upon. The basement meeting room has all of the latest anti-spy software, and we are unable to listen to any secret meetings being held in this basement location. Our final comment is that something of interest seems to be going on in the secure basement area, in that our sensors indicate much activity.

We have taken full photographs of all persons entering the twin towers from outside and have matched facial profiles with FBI files that you have made available to us.

We have found that fourteen of the one hundred and seventy-seven persons entering the building when Mr. da Vinci is in residence have been positively identified as persons of interest (also known as organized crime associates).

In place of our not being able to give more precise details of the meetings going on in the basement level location, we, as follows, give you a detailed report on the Century Towers buildings, in which da Vinci Enterprises appears to have an ownership interest.

§

Century City is a 176-acre neighborhood located on the west side of the Greater Los Angeles area. The neighborhood was developed on the former back lot of film studio 20th Century Fox. The area was offically opened up for business in 1963.

There are two private schools, but no public schools listed as being in the neighborhood. Most important to the local economy are a shopping center, twin business towers and the Fox Studios lot.

The land of Century City originally belonged to cowboy superstar Tom Mix (1880–1940), who used the location as a private ranch. It later became a back lot of 20th Century Fox Studios, which still has its headquarters there.

In 1956, Spyrus Skouras (1893–1971), who served as president of 20th Century Fox Studios from 1942 to 1963, and his nephew-in-law Edmond Herrscher (died 1983), an attorney, decided to develop the land for real-estate investments. The following year, in 1957, they commissioned a master plan development from Welton Becker Associates, which was unveiled at a major press event on the "western back lot" later that year.

In 1961, after 20th Century Fox suffered a string of expensive flops at movie-theater box offices, the studio tried unsuccessfully to make a comeback with its production of the movie *Cleopatra* whose twin stars were the sensation of Hollywood at that time. This movie had Elizabeth Taylor and Richard Burton as its two lead actors but the movie still did not do well.

The studio had to sell off its land in Century City for three hundred million dollars, which allowed it to pay its debts and show an interesting profit to its screaming stockholders.

The new owners conceived Century City as a city within "the city," and in 1963 opened up the buildings and retail stores for business. In 1966 the Century City Plaza Hotel opened for business, and has been the landmark structure for the area ever since.

Two famous movies were made within the confines of the city streets. Tbey were *A Guide to the Married Man* and *Conquest of the Planet of the Apes.*

– END REPORT –

§

Charlie had just finished putting away the paperwork from the field agents on the Century City report, when Sweetpea called and told him that she would be in his office in about twenty minutes. She said that she just received a response from the FBI on a perfect match of several pictures she had forwarded to them that the "Laurel and Hardy" team had turned in.

They were definitely organized crime matchups, and they were seen going into the da Vinci building in Century City, and it had to be Leonardo da Vinci that they were seeing, since there was no other known connection there. "Laurel and Hardy" were standing by at the only entrance and exit area to see when they would be leaving the building. It was hoped that they would be in the company of da Vinci, and if so, that would give them enough of a link between da Vinci and the Organization to get a court order for a search warrant.

A breathless Sweetpea arrived with one of the clerks from the Fereral Judges' office, who was prepared to give them a court order for a search and seizure of evidence from Century City if da Vinci could be photographed in the company of one of the two "made men."

The Federal clerk went to the lunch area, where he said he

would be for a while and to contact him if something concrete came up.

Sweetpea brought Charlie information on the good luck that Joe Wahl had earlier that morning downtown in the shopping area of the Alley.

He was just casually walking around accompanied by two undercover Sheriff's Deputies. One of the Deputies was a very nicely dressed female agent, who was carrying an obviously expensive Louis Vuitton handbag and stopping at several of the open-air market stalls to look at what they were selling.

Joe and the other deputy walked slowly behind her as so many other guys were doing, as they followed their wives or girlfriends down the busy walkways.

As they slowly continued walking and talking, they were approached by a nicely dressed young Hispanic man who told them that he had some high-end handbags and some expensive Cartier watches that they might want to look at.

While Joe was paying for one of the nice-looking knockoff hand bags that the deputy had selected, their other male companion stepped into the back room while the young guy and another person paid attention to the cash sale that was going on in front of them.

Joe was giving them a hard time and making problems over the change for the hundred-dollar bills he had given them for the purchase they were making.

When Joe was flashed the prearranged signal from his male deputy in the back room, he stopped the discussion on the purchase and pulled out his wallet with his badge attached, and their discussion over the money ended immediately. The seller knew that he was suddenly involved in the kind of undercover sting operation that he was always being warned about by his fellow street hustlers.

Joe and the female deputy quietly escorted the male Hispanic, whose name was Ricardo Lopez, into the back room as they dismissed the female, who was the one trying to make change for Joe. Within a matter of minutes Ricardo Lopez was placed under arrest for possession of illegal narcotics that the deputy had found in the back room.

A few quick questions asked of Ricardo gave them the answers they were looking for, and they arrested him right on the spot and moved him and the evidence to their car that was parked on the street.

Ricardo told them that the narcotics were supplied to most of the vendors by the Italian landlords, who split the profits with them on a fifty-fifty basis once the cost was taken off. Ricardo, who seemed to be a friendly and very talkative fellow, said that on a good day he would make $50 selling watches and purses and $300 as his percentage for selling packaged narcotics.

Ricardo said that he would tell them everything if they would let him go. Joe said he would see what he could do, but that they would need a written statement from him telling them all about how the supplier of the drugs worked with him.

Ricardo was taken downtown and booked into a holding cell where Sweetpea would get a statement from him that hopefully would lead them to a tie-in with the Mob and possibly with Mr. da Vinci himself.

Charlie was very pleased. He had Laurel and Hardy waiting to tie in da Vinci with some FBI-identified Mob guys, and he had Joe bringing in a front-line seller of narcotics from the Alley, where the connection to organized crime was a proven fact of life in L. A. Things were looking up.

CHAPTER FORTY-THREE

And then they got the break of breaks, or, as Joe Wahl would say, "If you set things up the right way, then all you have to do is wait."

The good luck that they were waiting for came later that afternoon, when Sweetpea took the call from the undercover agents in the field who were working the Century City stakeout. Laurel and Hardy told her, and she told Joe Wahl who was sitting there near her, and then Joe called Charlie and told him. After all the telephone tag, the bottom line was that if someone had granted the Sheriff's Department a wish for something that they really wanted, it actually happened.

The dynamic duo told them that Leonardo da Vinci XVIII had actually walked out of the front lobby and into the street with the two known Organization guys. He then gave each of them a hug, shook their hands and went his separate way. He would not have walked away with such a spring to his step and a great big smile on his handsome face if he had known that he had just been recorded on two separate cameras, from two separate views, hugging the two people who would connect him to the Cosa Nostra and give Charlie and all the agencies that he was connected with an opening to get their search warrants and go through the buildings, pulling up evidence that would eventually lead to the downfall of organized crime within the city limits of Los Angeles, California.

It also wouldn't hurt Charlie to have the future arrests and resulting information of major crimes operations on his record as leading the team that broke things wide open. Charlie had always dreamed about becoming the number-one man in the department, which would be the man sitting in the Sheriff's seat.

But for the moment, with none of the future's promise in anyone's thoughts, Charlie instructed Sweetpea to get together with the Legal Council's representative, who was waiting for someone to tell him what was needed for search warrants, etc..

Charlie was now able to shift the gears of the Sheriff's Department Operations to an all-out-war on the unsuspecting bad guys. Life was good, and Charlie knew it.

CHAPTER FORTY-FOUR

The operation to forcefully enter the twin towers was going to be ready to go down for next Sunday. That was three days from the morning meeting that was now being held in Charlie's office at the Sheriff's headquarters building. Charlie, Joe, Roberto and Sweetpea were sitting with Sergeant Ron Sellz of the Sheriff's Department's weapon and enforcement detail, the SWAT team.

Joe conducted the meeting and kept everything simple. He stressed that secrecy was absolutely vital, and if everything could stay unknown to everyone outside of this room, the chances of anyone getting injured would be greatly decreased.

The SWAT team would be handed the legal documents that Sweetpea was having prepared to allow them to "enter, search and seize" any and all documents deemed as important to the operation.

Sweetpea would give Sergeant Sellz the required paperwork to make the entry and arrest of anyone inside the building on that Sunday morning. She also instructed the Sergeant to obtain and provide a large enough lockable safe on wheels so that his men could secure all firearms, legal and all other paperwork, and anything else of interest.

She stressed again that the two areas of urgency were to be secured immediately; they were the entire penthouse area and the lower basement. It was the da Vinci operation in both locations that they were interested in. All persons found in the building on this Sunday morning, including front desk and security guards, were to be taken to headquarters for questioning. At no time was anyone other than his SWAT team to have any means of contacting outsiders. This meant that all cell phones and security in-house communication devises were to be immediately taken.

And most important, the security control room for the building, located on the third floor, was to be the prime target of the first deputies entering the building. They needed to keep the security room out of business during their entire operation, which they estimated would take most of the day.

The meeting ended with the understanding by everyone present that they would all meet here in Charlie's office at midnight Saturday evening and be ready to roll out with their fully armed men at first sunlight Sunday morning.

The meeting broke up with everyone giving and getting hugs all around. There was a definite air of nervousness and excitement over the upcoming course of action.

After everyone had left Charlie's office, Sweetpea stayed behind to help him put the paperwork in order, and then helped him lock everything back into the safe. They had previously agreed to have an early lunch together, and then go back to Sweetpea's apartment for the rest of the afternoon and evening.

§

As he ran his hands in a brief caress, he once again determined that her shoulders were straight and almost mannish, her breasts were full and high, and her hips were slender but generously curved. What more could one ask of so willing a female?

She rose on tiptoe to fully mold herself against his large and powerful frame. Her mouth opened to receive the heated branding of his searching tongue. A soft moan escaped her lips as she felt a simmering heat in the very depths of her being.

Charlie's ears were filled with the soft sounds coming from deep within her throat as he held her crushed against him. Charlie was tasting the softness of her cheek, the fragile curve of her jaw, and the slim line of her throat.

As he placed moist kisses along the upper edge of her shoulders, he felt the straining fullness of her breasts. He lowered his lips and placed feathery kisses between the valley created by her breasts, while his fingers brushed against the hardened tips.

The girl inhaled sharply as she felt the soft caress of his fingers going down her spine. But she released her held breath just as quickly as his head lowered once again down to her breasts. Sheer carnal desire flamed throughout her body as his lips settled over one rose-colored nipple. As he suckled the tender tip, her limbs weakened, and she felt herself slipping to the floor.

Before she could fall very far, Charlie gathered her up in his arms, and stepped carefully into the small alcove that contained her large bed. Gently he laid her down upon the rumpled coverlet.

His mouth consumed hers with its searching demand as his tongue pushed forward, and finding no resistance from the compliant female, he sought out and touched each and every curve of her body, as he once again traced a tempting path down to her ever-waiting breast. As he drew a sweet nipple into his mouth, her body trembled with a deep, wanton desire that left her clutching at his head and pressing herself fully against him.

It seemed only seconds later that she lay upon the coverlet with nothing covering her body. Her gown had been discarded upon the floor beside the bed, and for a breathless moment, Charlie stared down at the wonderful curves of perfection that he could see in the darkened room.

The heated flames within his eyes seared every inch of her flesh as he gazed down upon the fullness of her twin globes with their dusty rose-colored buds. His eyes roamed down the length of her trim rib cage to the tiny indent of her navel, across the womanly flare of her hips, and down the long shapely legs.

Charlie had bedded down a fair share of girls so far in his lifetime, but Sweetpea was so very special. He drew himself halfway up, eyes filling with burning desire as he looked down upon the junction of her womanhood, with the feathering of dark, curling hair lending a definite contrast to the creamy pearl iridescence of her skin.

As his eyes returned to her face, she was parting her lips as if to speak, but seeing the desire in his eyes, she was content and said nothing. The irresistible pull of pleasure's promise grabbed her body as Charlie's mouth again roamed over her. With feathered kisses, licking and nibbling, he ravished her breasts once again. His straight white teeth caressed her flesh and drove her mad with her own desire.

A soft moan escaped from her, deep within her throat, and at the same time his dark head lowered to her ribs, and the tempting curves of her waist and hips. The taste of her sweet flesh and the feel of her satin-smooth body combined to seduce Charlie into a physical wanting that knew no bounds. His hands splayed over the firmness of her belly, and then pressed on closer to her hips. His tongue sent flames shooting throughout the lower portion of her body, as he rubbed the inside of her thighs.

As his mouth touched her woman's jewel, she bucked as sweet, forbidden pleasure snaked through her womb and thrashing limbs. Without mercy, Charlie kept up his loveplay, his tongue plunging into her moist, sweet depths and lingering over the extremely sensitive nub as she shuddered again and again. Her cries filled his ears and fueled his desire to pleasure her to the fullest.

As the trembling of her body slowly subsided, and the fingers within his hair lessened their tight hold, Charlie rose from his position between her thighs. His lips seared branding kisses over her body as he finally pressed his length of manhood against her. His eyes witnessed the sated passion on her face before he covered her mouth once more with his own.

The girl opened up to him, too swept up in the steaming rapture of the moment to do otherwise. As Charlie's tongue filled her mouth, he felt the sculptured marble head of his "love-tool" pressing at the opening between her parted thighs.

His buttocks drew upward, and as he entered her, just an inch or so, he felt the tightness of her passage. Another thrust and another inch as he felt the velvet trembling of her inner sanctum. A low rumbling came from within his own chest and filled the entire room with his animal-like noises.

He moved back and forth, going slowly deeper and deeper, and then withdrawing back to the very lips of her moist opening. Over and over he plied her with his skillful seduction until she was clutching his back with her head thrown back wildly as the fullness in her loins drove her toward a frenzy of mindless desire. Each time the brand of his lance drove into her depths and stirred her, her body moved toward completion. Her legs slowly rose and fell as she sought to capture and hold onto the entire length of him that was deep within her.

Still holding himself back somewhat, Charlie caught hold of her buttocks, and with a talent born of past love-making, he maintained his inner control. Even as he felt the shuddering coming from the lady beneath him, he was able to inhale deep breaths of air, willing himself not to release the final fury of his passion. Charlie knew the power of her climax, and for a moment or two he fought his own heated need that was racing through his own loins. He watched her passion-filled face and heard the climatic moans escaping from her throat. Each thrust was now torture-laced for him as he fought off the aching need for his own fulfillment.

Only when he felt her climax receding did he allow himself to give vent to his own desire. His mouth covered hers, and as he plunged just a fraction deeper into her soft velvety depths, wildfire absolutely caught within him. Scalding pleasure burst forth from the center of his being, and showered upward, racing through his most powerful lance.

It took Charlie several minutes to regain his normal breathing and to conquer the disbelief that filled his brain as he thought about the wonderful moment that had just occurred between himself and his wonderful Sweetpea. A final shudder coursed through him as he realized that he had never before been driven to such powerful feeling of lust, and surely, he thought, she must have felt the same thing.

Turning his face so that he could gaze into her eyes, he found her eyelids closed, her breathing soft, and her arms caressing his neck. She slept peacefully in his arms, and a small smile filtered over his lips. Sleep, slow and pleasant came to him in the most wonderful manner.

All was quiet within the darkened room.

CHAPTER FORTY-FIVE

It was Sunday morning, a little bit after sunrise, which made it about six-twelve AM.

SWAT Chief Roberto Sanchez had assembled two hundred officers around the corner and out of sight of the entrance. They were on standby and were waiting on their orders to proceed to their predetermined locations within the Century City Towers Building. Their instructions were to secure the top-floor da Vinci offices, the third-floor communications center, and all of the basement locations. They were to put under immediate arrest and remove from the area all persons found within the building.

Standing by off to the side where they were out of the way of the bunched-up SWAT teams were lead Detective Charlie Glass and his number two, Detective Joe Wahl.

The agreed-upon plan was that two uniformed Sheriff's Deputies would walk up to the locked outer doors and gain entrance to the lobby area. Once inside, they were to arrest whoever it was that opened the doors for them. They were to be arrested, booked and taken away from the area as the rest of the two hundred officers would quickly rush in and move onto their pre-arranged assignment areas.

Following the wave of Charlie's hand signal to SWAT Chief Roberto Sanchez, the two officers walked slowly down the sidewalk that led to the front door of the Century City Tower Building. One of them took his baton from his holding belt and banged it against the locked glass door to get the attention of someone inside who would be able to open the door for them.

Moments later, one of the security guards, whose jacket read National Security Company, came to the door and opened it up from the inside for the two officers to step inside. As soon as the door was opened, one of the two officers took the National Security Company representative to the side of the doorway, where he told him quietly not to make any sudden moves or sounds, and that he was under arrest. He patted him down and found that he was carrying no weapon of any sort. He told the man to sit down facing away from the door, so that he was not able to see the rush of Sheriff's Officers moving rapidly into the lobby and onto the bank of elevators that would take them up to the penthouse and down to the third and basement levels.

Charlie, Joe Wahl and Roberto Sanchez were listening carefully to the two-way radio that kept them advised as to the progress of the deputies as they moved to their assigned areas.

On the penthouse floor there was no one in sight to let them into the officers, so the standard Swat Battering Ram was brought forward to smash in the locked outer glass door. The battering ram was an interesting piece of carved wood that fit over the right shoulder of two officers, who with practice were able to run at full speed together, crash into a doorway and cause the doorway to fall inward, allowing access to whatever was on the other side of the door.

Charlie told Joe Wahl when he saw the two-man battering ram being taken into the building a few minutes earlier that he had an interesting personal memory regarding a battering-ram situation that he was personally involved in many years ago when he first joined the Department.

Charlie and Jumbo Watson, a three-hundred-twenty-five-pound mountain of a man, were going to make an arrest at a bookmaking operation that was working out of a first-level garden apartment. The two officers could see into the apartment through a small side window that was open at the top for ventilation. They knew that they had to get into the bookie parlor, which was on the other side of the door that they knew was always locked, so they went to their squad car and got their two-man battering ram.

Jumbo was the front man and Charlie the back. They stood in the hallway outside the door and the two of them slowly together counted ONE, and they rocked back and forth, TWO, and they rocked back and forth again, and then on THREE, they charged forward, expecting to crash into the locked door that would give them entrance to the bookmaking room.

Just as they got to the door on the count of THREE, someone on the inside pulled the door open from the inside, probably planning to step into the outside hallway, and Charlie and Jumbo could not stop their forward momentum and ended up running right through the living room where all the bookmakers, who were sitting at little desks with a telephone on each one, watched the two cops as they flew through the room and out the open sliding door and into the connecting pool with a huge splash.

By the time Charlie and Jumbo got themselves out of the pool and took their dripping-wet bodies into the apartment, everyone was gone, including the gambling slips that probably got flushed down the toilets.

Charlie and Jumbo had great fun telling and retelling that story to anyone at the station house who would listen.

And Charlie had to smile to himself as he saw the two-man battering ram being rushed over to the building. He was thinking that many things would change over the years, but something like the two-man battering ram would be around forever.

§

Things began to move rapidly once the front door had been opened.

Men and materials poured into the lobby. Each Sheriff's Deputy carried a standard issue sidearm, which was a 9-millimeter pistol or a .38 special revolver. Each weapon carried lots of firepower. As a backup, every Sheriff's patrol car carried a 12-gauge shotgun for heavy-duty work.

The men were broken up into three equal groups and one floating group. The penthouse and the two basement areas would have sixty men for each location. The remaining twenty or so deputies would roam about the various floors and offices to see if there was anyone that they had missed during the original sweep of the various floors.

Charlie and Joe Wahl were still outside waiting for the all-clear signal to be given so that they could enter the building and proceed with their plan of action.

It was over an hour before everyone found inside the Century City Tower building was arrested and loaded into Sheriff's Department transportation vans and taken away. Most of the persons found were security guards, some plumbers, and cleaning crews. They would be held for several hours until the operation came to a close and then released. It was believed that no telephone calls or any other form of communication had left the building, and that they could go forward in an organized and proper manner.

It was decided that the order of procedure would be to start at the communication center on the third floor, then go down to the lower basement, followed by the upper basement, and finally the penthouse, which they all believed would be the most interesting place of all. The required investigation book was being kept by SWAT leader Roberto Sanchez, who made notes upon each and every room that they went into and what they saw there, and he tagged and labeled each item that was taken away.

The third-floor communication center held nothing of interest for them, and the group of three, Roberto Sanches, Joe Wahl and

Charlie Glass, each signed off that nothing of interest was located there and they moved on. The lower basement, which was labeled as Sub-Basement One, gave up nothing but stored records and furniture for the building. The area was also signed off.

It was the second basement, to which they gave the label of Sub-Basement Two, that gave them a taste of what they were looking for. The huge area was full of unlocked doors to rooms that held various items of no interest. But it was in the very back of Sub-Basement Two that a huge locked door prevented them from entering. A very professionally printed metal sign told everyone, "THIS ROOM HOLDS PRIVATE BUSINESS RECORDS FOR THE DA VINCI ENTERPRISE CORPORATION. ENTRY IS FORBIDDEN UNLESS ESCORTED BY DA VINCI PERSONNEL." It asked anyone who had a need to enter the area to please report their request to the reception area in the penthouse.

One of the SWAT Team members used a bolt cutter and cut off the security lock on the door. There was also a large combination lock, and rather than take the time to figure out the combination, Roberto Sanchez had one of his men put a good-sized explosive device over the lock area, and when the rooms were completely clear of everyone, he gave the order to blow the lock off. The area was cleared and the order was given. The explosion went off with a large *whop* and a bang as the now-unlocked door swung open. Huge blowing fans were brought in, and the dust and dirt that were now all over everything were cleared out of the room.

The first thing that they saw when they entered the large room was a gun rack that took up one entire side wall. There were possibly fifty weapons or more, and the Sheriff's Deputies wore gloves so as not to mix in their prints with others. The hope was that these weapons would give up the persons who might have used them during the commission of a crime or other criminal activities. The inventory was amazingly deep into heavy-duty weapons, and Roberto Sanchez recorded each make, model and serial number for every weapon and for the ammunition that went with them.

There were many illegally modified automatic weapons with high firepower and scopes, and several AK-47 rifles! There were a few smaller Beretta pistols and a few .38 special revolvers. It was a tremendous arsenal and everyone was getting excited, as they knew that they were into something big.

CHAPTER FORTY-SIX

It took several hours to write up, record and load up the evidence boxes with the firearms, and finally Roberto Sanchez officially closed off the Sub-Basement Two area and left several deputies on that level to keep everyone out.

The next order of business was to move the operation to the penthouse of da Vinci Enterprises. Roberto Sanchez had stationed six deputies outside of the penthouse doors leading into the offices in order to keep the area clear of any and all outside interference.

When Roberto, Joe and Charlie stepped off the elevator that placed them outside the glass doorway of the da Vinci offices, they found everything quiet, and that no one had gone in or out of the closed offices according to the officers who were stationed there. Not having keys to open up the huge glass doors that were labeled DA VINCI ENTERPRISES, Roberto Sanchez ordered up the two-man battering-ram team, who made short order of the resistance offered by the doors. It took longer to clean up and take away the broken glass from the doors than it had to knock them down.

The offices were divided into different sections, with three different hallways going in opposing directions leading away from the reception desk, which dominated the room.

They all agreed that they all would stay together as they searched each location, and they began with the opening of each drawer from the reception desk. They piled all the pens, papers, notepads, etc. on top of the desk, and determining that there was nothing of interest to be learned from them, they turned their attention to hallway number one, which was to the extreme left of the room.

There was a middle hallway, and then finally the hallway on the extreme right, which Charlie remembered walking down to the da Vinci office. It was the da Vinci office that had the best chance of giving up something of great interest and it would be the last place looked at.

The first and second hallways gave up small side offices that had nothing of interest to offer, and it was not more that thirty minutes later that the three of them stood inside the entrance to Mr. Big's personal location.

Slowly and in great detail, Charlie reviewed the conversation that he had with da Vinci with Joe Wahl and Roberto Sanchez. He explained how he had just decided to walk in and put a little pressure on the man. Everybody reacts differently to pressure, and he wanted to see how da Vinci responded.

It was his referring to Captain Crewe that locked in da Vinci as the bad guy. If he had not panicked and called the captain as quickly as he had, then he might have slipped away. But he did call, and then little bits and pieces started to fall in place—like one of the three City Hall shooters knowing da Vinci's name.

Charlie said that he couldn't wait to look at things in the penthouse and he described da Vinci's great taste in personal secretaries. The one that he had seen was a real looker. He told them, because neither of them had ever seen da Vinci, that this Leonardo was well-dressed, good-looking and physically a very dominant alpha male.

The three of them walked the same long hallway that led to the da Vinci offices. Without him sitting behind the desk, the room looked a lot smaller to Charlie. His desk was unlocked and everything that they poured from it filled the desk top, but there was really nothing of interest there.

Roberto got down on his hands and knees and crawled forward until he was completely out of sight as he squeezed himself into the opening between the side drawers and where a person's legs would slide under the desk if they were seated. Charlie and Joe watched as he reappeared again—only this time he was holding a little black book that must have been taped to the underside of the leg space. The book was small, possibly three inches by four inches and Roberto was holding it above his head and laughing.

When he was back on his feet, he rolled the chair over that went with the desk, and he sat down. Not a word was spoken as Charlie and Joe watched Roberto open the little black book and slowly began to turn the pages. He lingered over the book for a few minutes and then handed it to Charlie who also flipped through it and gave it over to Joe. The three of them looked at each other and burst out laughing.

All of them were sure that they had something here that was going to break open the case, but it wasn't going to be that easy after all. It would have been great if that little black book turned out to be a code book of some kind, with names and numbers that would have laid out the case for them and would lead them on to ultimate victory.

That was not going to happen. The little black book had a total of fourteen pages in it and each page had one large letter printed in the very center of the page.

Roberto took out his personal note book and printed out in large block letters what each of the fourteen letters spelled out,

It read F-U-C-K-Y-O-U-C-O-P-P-E-R-S!

CHAPTER FORTY-SEVEN

It was nine o'clock the next morning, and Sweetpea had joined the three detectives who were sitting together in the Sheriff's Headquarters lunch room. They had the room to themselves as Sweetpea served them all coffee and some dessert choices.

Surprisingly, they were all in a good mood. It was not very often that they were outsmarted at every turn, and as Joe Wahl said, if he were wearing a hat, he would take it off to Mr. Leonardo da Vinci. It wasn't every day that the entire Sheriff's Department was suckered, but yesterday was that day.

They had gone through the motions and followed proper procedure when they opened up several wall safes in the da Vinci office. What they found in each of the safes was the very same letter, addressed to each of the three lead detectives. Obviously Leonardo da Vinci had an inside connection somewhere high up in their very own Sheriff's Department, and this was the one part that had them all worried. The insider, or the "worm" as Joe Wahl called him or her, was obviously a highly placed person who had access to all the records and paperwork on the case and was right up to the moment!

It was time to open the letter addressed to each of them that they had found in the da Vinci safe inside his offices. The letter in each of the three envelopes was addressed to Charlie Glass—Joe Wahl—Roberto Sanchez.

It read as follows:

CHARLES GLASS – LEAD DETECTIVE
JOE WALES – SECOND POSITION TEAM DETECTIVE
ROBERTO SANCHEZ – SWAT

Gentlemen:

I would like to issue an apology for the vulgarity in the words I used for the inside of the little black book that by now you have located from the hiding place under my desk top. I could not resist writing out those three little words, and I hope you can laugh with me. I am only sorry that I could not see the look on your faces when, expecting names, dates and other things in the book, you found the three little words I left for you. I only hope that the three of you can laugh with me at my little joke, even though the joke was on you.

Obviously, you realize that I have physically removed my operation from the Century City Towers and have gone into my backup mode. I am still in the greater Los Angeles city area and will remain here until I finish up some open business matters that need to be concluded.

I enjoyed meeting you, Detective Glass, when you paid your social call on me at my office recently. It was time to rid myself of Captain Crewe, in that he was becoming a pain in the butt. He is all yours but I must tell you that he really knows nothing about my operation. Kindly send him my regards.

Once I tie up a few loose ends in the city, I will be long gone. I plan to travel in Europe for a while and then settle in somewhere in Italy where they really appreciate Italian-American gangsters (as our friend the good Captain Crewe used to call me and my associates.)

And finally, I'm positive that you all laughed when it became known that I claimed a direct line to my ancestor, the original and great Leonardo da Vinci, who lived during the European Renaissance era.

In closing, let me clear up the question that must still linger in your minds as to why I ordered my three city hall shooters to die. Even though we only "got" two out of three, it does not matter any more. You see, the reason I wanted them removed was that their handler (whom I have since punished) dropped my name in a telephone conversation that they overheard.

And now, since you know who and what I am, the death of the third shooter doesn't matter anymore, and I assure you that he is in no danger from my organization.

I wish to close this note, which seems to be a lot longer than I had originally planned, with the comment that even though people laugh at my claim of a direct family tie to the great Leonardo, I assure you that my claim is correct.

I wish to leave you all with a final puzzzle. Obviously there is a traitor in your midst, and he or she was planted there many years ago so that I would always know what was going on in the sheriff's department.

I have cut off all ties with this person, and even if you get lucky and do find him or her, it will not matter to me. I wish you all good hunting.

Very truly yours,
Leonardo da Vinci XVIII

CHAPTER FORTY-EIGHT

It was at dinner that night that a depressed Charlie had calmed down enough to talk about "the letter" with Sweetpea.

Charlie had abruptly ended the morning's meeting after they all had read the da Vinci letter. Everyone had left in a somber mood, and each of them went their separate way. It was only Sweetpea to whom Charlie could turn to and express his feelings and frustrations at the way the Mulholland murder case was twisting and turning.

While they were waiting to be seated at Dupar's Restaurant, located inside the L.A. Farmers Market, Charlie walked over to an interesting-looking storyboard and started to read. It was so interesting that he called Sweetpea over and told her to take a look at a bit of the history of the Farmers Market that hardly anyone knew.

Moments later, the two of them were reading and enjoying the storyboard:

HISTORICAL FACTS ABOUT THE WORLD-FAMOUS FARMERS MARKET—
LOCATED AT 3RD AND FAIRFAX IN CENTRAL LOS ANGELES, CALIFORNIA.

In 1880, A.F. Gilmore and a partner bought two dairy farms in the central Los Angeles area. The parners decided to split their holdings ten years later, and Mr. Gilmore took control of the large 256-acre ranch, its dairy herd and farmhands, at what is now the world-famous corner of 3rd and Fairfax.

When Mr. Gilmore wanted to expand his dairy herd, he started drilling new wells for needed water. Instead of water, he discovered oil, and the dairy herd was quickly replaced by a large field of oil derricks. The Gilmore property remained very productive into the 1930s, when the Great Depression hit the area.

Two local businessmen, Fred Beck and Roger Dahlhjelm, approached the son of Mr. Gilmore who had passed away. They wanted to build a "village" at the corner of 3rd and Fairfax where local farmers could sell their fresh produce on a daily basis.

In July of 1934, a dozen farmers parked their trucks there and began to sell their produce from the back of their vehicles. Word spread, and in a few years permanent buildings and selling stalls popped up until today, 3rd and Fairfax has become a must-see location for travelers from around the entire world.

Hollywood and Farmers Market have been extremely good friends for years and years.

Shirley Temple, the nation's early top box-office draw, always gathered a large adoring crowd at Brock's Candy Store, where she liked to hang out.

Pictures of Ava Gardner trying on hats at Dell's Hat Shop were shown in all of the local papers.

Marilyn Monroe appeared early in her career as "Miss Cheesecake" of 1953, when she helped open up Michael's Cheesecake Store.

Movie stars shared their affection with Farmers Market with other luminaries of the day

President Dwight Eisenhower admired the peanut-butter machine at Magee's Nut Store.

A few years later, the Beatles visited the same store.

And finally, the incomparable singer, Frank Sinatra, was pals with Patsy d'Amoro of Patsy's Pizza Shop in Farmers Market.

§

Sweetpea and Charlie were finally seated in the very rear of the large restaurant, where it would be quieter than the usual restaurant noise. Charlie was tapping the da Vinci letter that he had brought with him on top of the water glass. He continued to tap at it until Sweetpea slipped it away from his fingers. They sat there in silence until the waiter came over and took their order.

It was Sweetpea who broke the silence. "Well, Charlie, what's our next step? Where do we go from here?"

Charlie, who had been doing a lot of silent thinking and gathering-up of his thoughts since they left the meeting that morning, didn't answer right away. Instead of speaking, he handed her a ball-point pen, a three-ring notebook and a package of 3x5 index cards. "Sweetpea, my love, you know me better than anyone else in the world, and I know that I have your trust and loyalty at all times. We have to be very careful at this point in the investigation. We have to keep our thoughts to ourselves, because if we don't, we won't survive this investigation that seems to get deeper and deeper and promises to swallow us up. I trust you, and you trust me, and that is as far as we go on any of this.

"I am going to call in the FBI to sit in with us on our investigation. They are not part of any of our local organizations and seem to be the only one that we can trust. I'm going to dictate to you now, and what I tell you is for you only to hear and write up, and then to forget it all. I want you to write this up and label it 'FOR THE EYES ONLY OF CHARLIE GLASS, DETECTIVE SECOND GRADE, SHERIFF'S DEPARTMENT, LOS ANGELES, CALIFORNIA.'

"Do not make a duplicate copy of what I dictate to you. I want only one original, and I want you to forget about what I am about to say after you write it down. For your protection, I am taking you out of the loop on this case.

"Your last act will be to type up these notes for me, and then to take a leave of absence. I want you to leave town for a few weeks and visit your sister in Chicago, and I don't want you to come back until I either send for you, or you hear through the Sheriff's Department that I am no longer among the living. This dictation I am going to give you now must go no further, and we shall not talk about it again until either the case is ended or I am.

"Now, I always think better when I see things set up in writing, so please take my words down exactly as I say them. To repeat, I will need to have your written copy of all of this, first thing in the morning, before you leave for Chicago. And now, here is what I have to say.

§

FOR THE EYES ONLY OF CHARLES GLASS, DETECTIVE SECOND GRADE - LOS ANGELES SHERIFF'S DEPARTMENT.

1) At this moment, it is very unclear as to who my immediate superior is within the Los Angeles Sheriff's Department. This is because Captain Crewe, to whom I have always reported, is presently in jail, and the charges have not been formalized as of yet.

The depth of the captain's involvement in the case of the Mulholland double murders is not clear right now, and needs to be resolved.

2) A very important question is, how much do I

trust my number two in command on this case. I originally suspected my partner, Joe Wahl, of being the original murderer of the double homicide from the Mulholland Drive case, and I thought that new evidence cleared him completely of all wrong doing.

The letter received by the suspect known as Leonardo da Vinci XVIII points a finger at his possible involvement in all of this.

With Joe Wahl being labeled as innocent by me, and then as possibly guilty again for a second time, a detailed look into this possibility is needed.

3) And if not Detective joe Wahl as a suspect, where does the SWAT team leader Roberto Sanchez fit into all this?

His information on the case seems to be better than mine, and there is no way that I can see how he has acquired so many details of what happened without being told. His superior knowledge of the investigation seems to be too good and too accurate for only being on the crime scene for such a short period of time.

4)All other persons connected to the case, starting with Sweetpea Soll from the Legal Department, several patrol persons, ambulance attendants, on-site reporters, the Los Angeles Police Department and other sheriff's department investigators— all were away from the beaten track and cannot be considered as suspects in any and all matters connected to the Mulholland and City Hall murders.

5) The murderous hit at City Hall that took out the political connections from the mayor's office was explained away by Captain Crewe as being incidental to the overall activities of organized crime. I see no further involvement of any other politician with the Mob and/or Leonardo da Vinci XVIII.

6) I realize that my personal hero, Captain Crewe, is very deeply involved in the case against organized crime and will be dealt with by due process of the law.

7) da Vinci's last letter pointed out that there was someone beyond the captain who helped him with insider information. It is this insider person that must be stopped, and this is the direction that this investigation will be taking.

§

End dictation of report by Detective Charlie Glass - Detective Second Grade - Los Angeles Sheriff's Department

CHAPTER FORTY-NINE

Three days had passed, and Sweetpea had taken her leave of absence and was on her way to visit relatives in Chicago as per Charlie's suggestion.

During the past two of those days, Charlie, unaccompanied by either Joe Wahl or Roberto Sanchez, had spent his time with Mel Kaplan from the Federal Bureau of Investigation. Mel Kaplan had given him several very detailed informative file folders on four of his highest-level Los Angeles investigators, who worked out of his office on Wilshire Boulevard in Westwood, California. There was a huge FBI presence in Southern California, and this huge complex dominated the entire area.

Charlie had gone over each file very carefully in order to be sure that none of these Federal agents had any ties to the L.A. Sheriff's Department. He had selected two of Mel Kaplan's top agents who had caught his eye for their ability to look deeper than their fellow investigators would look at whatever it was that they were working on. The two FBI investigating agents who seemed to stand out from the rest of the offerings were Alberta Wallack and Jerry Sloan.

Alberta Wallack, an attractive female person of color, and Jerry Sloan, a tall and awkward-looking Caucasian guy, had both been with the FBI for about twelve years each. They had won awards working together on two very special government cases as silent and invisible intelligence investigators, doing the behind-the-scenes legal discovery that is so important to government cases at such a high level.

It was a quiet and secretive manner that Charlie was looking for, and they seemed perfect for the role. If the Sheriff's Department was going to be involved in an internal scandal, then Kaplan and Sloan seemed to be perfectly suited for keeping things to themselves. Mel Kaplan, Senior Assignment Manager for the Los Angeles Federal Bureau Investigation Unit, assigned Alberta Wallace and Alan Sloan to Charlie forthwith. The three of them agreed that they should never be seen together, and their meeting place was to be Sweetpea Soll's apartment, which was located in a central downtown Los Angeles converted loft.

Charlie told the interesting story behind Sweetpea's downtown L.A. loft apartment, which was located on 9th Street and Figueroa just west of central downtown. She took the apartment loft because it was only a ten-minute walk up Figueroa Street to the Sheriff's Department where she worked. Walking to work in Los Angeles is a luxury that not many people have.

Charlie explained to them that the Original Pantry Café is an iconic coffee shop and restaurant in Los Angeles, on the corner of 9th Street and Figueroa Street in downtown L.A.'s South Park district.

The "Pantry" (as it is known by locals) claims to never have been closed or being without a customer since it opened its doors, including when it changed locations in 1950 to make room for a freeway off-ramp. It served lunch at the old location and dinner at the new location on the same day. The restaurant is currently owned by former Los Angeles mayor Richard Riordan and has served many celebrities and politicans.

When it was opened in 1924, the restaurant consisted of one room, a fifteen-stool counter, a small grill, a single hot plate and such. It has been designated as Los Angeles Historical-Cultural

Monument #255, and has been ranked as the most famous restaurant in the entire Los Angeles area.

The restaurant is known for serving cole slaw to all patrons in the evening hours, even if they ultimately decide to order breakfast instead. It claims to serve ninety tons of bread (461 loaves per day) and ten and a half tons of coffee per year.

The two FBI agents got their keys, and it was agree that Kaplan and Sloan would use FBI equipment before any of their meetings to electronically sweep the apartment for listening devices of any sort.

It was decided that the undercover operation would be divided into two separate parts, and each would be dealt with separately. Each would be an ongoing operation, but only going after Leonardo da Vinci would be an out-in-the-open investigation that would involve Roberto Sanchez and Joe Wahl.

§

Alberta Walllack and Jerry Sloan were introduced to Roberto and Joe at a meeting called the next day after everything was set up between Charlie and the special investigative unit from the FBI.

It was explained that Charlie had asked for the help of the Feds because they were the ones who would officially be in charge of the investigation of the international crime organization. The Sheriff's Department had very limited abilities outside the jurisdiction of Los Angeles County.

Charlie passed out four of the five sets of information and kept one for himself. They would take a few minutes to read and digest the short report.

CHAPTER FIFTY

L.A. CRIME FAMILY INFORMATION

The Los Angeles crime family is an Italian-American criminal organization based in Southern California as part of the American Mafia (Cosa Nostra). Since its inception in the early 1900s, it has spread throughout the Southern California area.

Like most Mafia families in the United States, the Los Angeles crime family gained power by its bootlegging in the early Prohibition era. The Los Angeles family reached its peak in the 1950s, 1960s and 1970s. The Los Angeles family was never as big as the New York or Chicago families.

Since 1980, the "RICO act" against criminal activites has been very effective in shrinking the American Mafia. The Los Angeles Mafia now holds only a small fraction of its former powers and has gone local in its dealings. Not having a strong concentration of Italian-Americans in Southern California, it leaves the family in a constant internal fight with the Los Angeles street gangs who now dominate the area.

This small Los Angeles crime family of Italians

is the last Mafia family left in the state of California.

Summary

This Los Angeles crime family was founded by Joseph Ardizzone in the year 1900 and has lasted until the present time. It has always limited its territory to Southern California and Las Vegas, Nevada. It is run and maintained by local members who are "made men," who must be Italian. Any members not pure Italian on both sides of their parental families are known as associates only.

Their criminal activities are usually racketeering, money laundering; murder, extortion, gambling, and drugs.

The local Mob has allies among the five other major Mafia families. These other five areas are Chicago, New York, Buffalo, Cleveland and Kansas City.

Their major rivals within Southern California are the many street gangs, who do the same illegal acts they have always done.

§

Specific background leading to the present crime families

While other Mafia families in the United States were prospering in the 1960s, the 1970s and on into the present 1980s, the Los Angeles family was beginning its major decline.

When William H. Parker became chief of

police in Los Angeles, the sheriff's department found someone that it could work hand in hand with in cracking down on organized crime in its jurisdiction. The weakened Los Angeles Mob had lost ground to the Chicago and New York organizations.

Due to over fifty-five unsolved gangland killings in the area, the local police forces combined their efforts and formed what was soon to be known as "the gangster squad." This was put together by Chief Parker as a group of investigators to harass the Los Angeles Mob family everywhere. They were so successful that membership in the Los Angeles Mafia fell to an all-time low of thirty members.

The only bright spot for the Mob during the "gangster squad" years was its operation called the "Roberta Dress Manufacturing Company." This was an unbreakable front that they used to absorb local unions into the fold, and the business continues on today,

In our own 1980s, Leonardo da Vinci XVIII was made official boss of the Los Angeles crime family. He moved the family heavily into narcotics, pornography, gambling, and loan-sharking.

Only recently has the name of Leonardo da Vinci XVIII come up as the kingpin of the Los Angeles crime family to the known world. A one-million-dollar-a-week bookmaking scheme keeps da Vinci personally involved. He is known to move his location around from area to area and has been difficult to find and arrest.

da Vinci has brought the Mob back to strength,

and they now stand independent of Las Vegas, Chicago or New York. At present da Vinci and his Mob associates have been taken off the radar of the Los Angeles Police Dcepartment and the Sheriff's Department due to the problems they are having with gangs in the Southern California area. This is giving the organization time to reorganize themselves with the unions and small business owners. It seems that da Vinci has made his peace with the local Russian gangs and the Chinese Triads who operate in the same areas.

While the Mob has not yet reached its full strength under da Vinci, we have agreed to work alongside the Sheriff's Department as they take the lead in the fight here in Southern California against the Organization.

End report – Cosa Nostra – AKA the Organization – AKA the Mob

CHAPTER FIFTY-ONE

Charlie had convinced himself that it would be impossible to attack both of his problems at the same time. He knew that he should deal with the da Vinci problem first and then follow up with the internal security issue. His reasoning was perfectly clear; at least, he thought that it was! By going after da Vinci he would still have full use of both Roberto and Joe—and he also would know where both of them were at all times.

He spoke to no one about his new idea about how to find Leonardo da Vinci XVIII where he was hiding out. He knew that he would still be in Los Angeles somewhere, since he was still conducting business. Finding him by the normal search-and-locate way would never work, because da Vinci would have himself buried several layers deep and would never be found using the conventional methods. However—and this was a big HOWEVER—Charlie had a new idea, a unique idea, and one that he never thought of using before and probably would never use again.

He made no comments to anyone, and took himself into the Sheriff's Department Historical Archives, where the entire case-by-case history of the Sheriff's and Los Angeles Police Departments' day-by-day historical events were kept under protective lockup. After showing his badge to the custodian, he was allowed into the dusty records room, where he was confident that he would find

208

what he was looking for. He thought that it was wonderful having full access to something he really wanted to see right there at his fingertips.

He wanted to know what the records said about the famous LAPD "Gangster Squad" that he remembered hearing so much about when he was a rookie and just breaking into "the job." The memory that he was searching for went way back to his first rookie year in the mid-1970s.

It took him all of the morning and well into the afternoon before he found what he was looking for. Using his police credentials, he was able to convince the machine to print out what he needed. He was very excited and impatient to see if his memory of what he would have in a few minutes would be what he hoped it was.

GANGSTER SQUAD

Restricted information file limited to Los Angeles Police Department and Sheriff's credentialed persons only.

§

The "Gangster Squad" (later known as the Organized Crime Intelligence Division, OCID), was a special unit created by the LAPD in 1946 to keep the East Coast Mafia and organized crime elements out of the Los Angeles area. It was created by then-Chief of Police Clemonce B. Horrall in 1946 as an eight-man intelligence detail. Along with fighting organized crime, they were given the job of spying on corrupt cops.

Criminals like Mickey Cohen, Jack Dragna, Bugsy Siegel, Jack Whalen and Jimmy Fratianno, to name a few, were targets that the Gangster Squad went after. They waged war on crime and did things that would be considered illegal in today's world.

The next LAPD Chief, William Parker, expanded the team in 1950, which then included a female field team. Chief Parker privately urged his Gangster Squad to go beyond the law when they thought vigilantism was necessary. He backed them everytime they would be brought up on charges for any excessive use of force. He charged them to embark upon an extra-legal campaign of surveillance, brutality and murder in order to save "his"city.

§

Sidebar note on personal side of Chief Willam H. Parker III.

In downtown Los Angeles in the year 1922, two very different men began their very different careers on both sides of the law.

William H. Parker III was a seventeen-year-old who had moved with his family to Los Angeles from Deadwood, South Dakota. He had a long-time job working as a movie usher in the Loews movie theatres

The other person in this comparison was a nine-year-old hoodlum who was about to commit his first violent crime: holding up a local store.

The bitter rivalry that showed up in later years between these two young men would shape the culture of the LAPD and the history of 20th-century

Los Angeles.

In 1927, Parker became a police officer. He was extremely intolerant of fools and was famously incorruptible in a department that was openly corrupt. Parker gradually rose up the ranks, and in 1950, a scandal involving 114 Hollywood "pleasure girls," made Parker the Chief of Police for his careful handling of the famous case. He would continue to hold this job for sixteen controversial years. In the often-quoted words of the *Los Angeles Times* publisher, Norman Chandler, "Parker was the most powerful man in Los Angeles."

And ... Mickey Cohen was born Meyer Harris Cohen in the Brownsville section of Brooklyn, New York, in 1913.

Mickey arrived in Los Angeles with his mother and sister at the age of three. By the age of six, he was hustling newspapers on the streets of Boyle Heights near downtown Los Angeles. One year later he was arrested for book making.

Mickey's talent with his fists took the diminutive brawler to New York City to train as a featherweight boxer. His great skill with a .38 revolver, however, took him into the big-time rackets, first in Cleveland, and then to Al Capone's Chicago.

In 1937, Mickey returned to Los Angeles to serve as gangster Bugsy Siegel's right-hand man. This was the job that took him on a collision course with Chief of Police William Parker.

For three decades, from the Great Depression to the Watts riots, Parker and Cohen, the policeman and the gangster, engaged in a struggle for power—

each as a lieutenant to older and more powerful men and then directly against each other. Their rivalry attracted the attention of a young United States Senator named Robert Kennedy, and the antagonism of FBI Director J. Edgar Hoover.

The struggle between the two enemies who were on different sides of the law involved some of the most powerful and colorful figures of the 20th century. The following famous names would take up the cause of one or the other of the two feuding men.

Newspapermen Harry Chandler and his nemesis William Randolph Hearst, studio head Harry Cohen of Columbia Studios, entertainers Jack Webb, Frank Sinatra, Lana Turner and Sammy Davis, Jr.

Civil rights leaders Malcom X and Martin Luther King, Jr., took the views of one side or the other in regards to the duelling police chief and the gangster.

END REPORT

CHAPTER FIFTY-TWO

Charlie had taken all his notes and copies of the printouts home with him and, for possibly the tenth time that night, had just sat there and read and re-read the detailed information on the former Police Chief of the Los Angeles Police Department, and how he formed the infamous Gangster Squad. He loved knowing the fact that a legal and original precedent had been set that he could follow.

This beloved former Director of the LAPD even had Police Headquarters named after him. Of course this was the Parker Center Police Offices, right in the middle of central Los Angeles's Financial District.

When Chief Parker decided to let the Gangster Squad continue to function, he was the highest-ranking officer, and he needed no one's permission to do so. He was able, at that particular moment in time, to do whatever he wanted, whenever he wanted, and there was no one who had enough authority to stop or even slow him down if they had wanted to.

In Charlie's case, his own superior officer, Captain Crewe, was absolutely unavailable to be asked for his viewpoint, since he was a resident of the jailhouse and out of any decision-making on anything except perhaps his own dinner choices. Charlie looked upon himself right now as the present reigning superior officer in charge of working the double murder case, and he believed that his decisions as lead officer would be upheld even if a review of his actions ever were to come up.

An interesting plan was forming in Charlie's head, and it seemed simple enough. There were two important things that he wanted to achieve before someone was placed in a senior position above him and could cut off his plans.

The hottest issue, which was burning a hole in everything that he was trying to achieve, was to accurately identify and eliminate the mole in his department. This guy was very smart and very slick and had out-thought them all every single time over many years. The mole knew everything that was going on around him in the Sheriff's Department, and yet was able to keep himself both informed and safe at all times. Getting to this guy was of the utmost importance, because any success that they might have on anything else that the Department went into would as always, depend on secrecy and security. So getting the mole was his number-one priority, but he had to put it into a number-two position.

He needed one of his suspects, Joe and Roberto, to reveal himself by being too good on getting to the hiding Leonardo da Vinci. He thought that whoever the mole was would use inside information on da Vinci's organization to make himself look good with arrests and procedures. In reality, Charlie was hoping that this insider knowledge would point out to him the one guy who knew much more than anyone else, and this would be evident by the number of arrests he would make based on that privileged knowledge. Right now everything was pointing at Joe Wahl; either he or Roberto would need to give themselves away, which so far they had not done.

Charlie needed to come up with a few twists and turns, and for that he knew that he needed Sweetpea and her legal department behind him. With a smile on his face and a great feeling in his heart about doing so, he would send her an "all clear and come on home" message. He was really looking forward to seeing her.

Things were looking interesting as he closed all the paperwork up and went to sleep.

CHAPTER FIFTY-THREE

Charlie was up very early the next morning and was at his desk at the Sheriff's Headquarters long before the sun was due to rise. He had with him the final readouts that he had requested on the final battles for power and control of Los Angeles under Chief Parker and his opposite number, the infamous crime boss Mickey Cohen. He wanted to review what he thought he had read about where Chief Parker had hired U.S. Marines and given them police badges after he had trained them, and turned them loose on organized crime as it was being run by kingpin Mickey Cohen.

Unless he missed something important, there was no reason he could not go out of the ranks of the local Sheriff's Department, as Chief Parker had many years before, and hire up a professional squad of trained "head-busters" to work with him on his da Vinci problem.

He had several pages to re-read on the history of Chief Parker and Mickey Cohen, and then some telephone calls that needed to be made in order to recruit the same kind of men used in those earlier days to break up the Mob. If it had worked for Chief Parker, there was no reason that it couldn't work again for him!

He opened up the first page of the report, thinking that with any luck, he could put together a squad of his own, based on the old "Gangster Squad" idea from Chief Parker.

There were two file folders and he decided he would read the one labeled "MICKEY COHEN" first. It was thicker than the other one labeled "WILLIAM PARKER – CHIEF OF POLICE.

§

Mickey Cohen, Gangster
Born September 4, 1913: Brooklyn, New York
Died July 29, 1976: Los Angeles, California
Nicknames: Irish Mickey, Gangster Mickey.
Known associates: Benjamin "Bugsy" Siegel; Meyer Lansky; the "Outfit"—the Organization; Jack Dragon; Candy Barr, exotic dancer; Johnny Stompanato

Like many gangsters of the day, Meyer Harry Cohen started out his life hustling newspapers on the streets of New York.

His Orthodox Jewish family moved from Brooklyn to Los Angeles when Mickey was nine years old. He quickly got into trouble and was sent to reform school, where he picked up amateur boxing skills.

When Mickey was fifteen, he moved to Cleveland in an effort to become a professional boxer and to compete in some minor matches. At the time, many fights were "fixed" and the outcome of the match was always known in advance!

On April 8, 1930, Mickey Cohen fought and won his first professional bout. This was also his last fight so he was honestly able to say that he never lost a professional boxing match in his entire life.

In Cleveland, Cohen met associates of Moe

Dalitz, a Midwestern bootlegger who would go on to become one of Las Vegas's leading casino operators. It was also in Cleveland that Cohen was first arrested for armed robbery. With the help of his new friends, he beat the rap and walked away.

Trying to avoid the scrutiny of the local police, who now had him on their radar, the young gangster moved to Chicago, where he went to work for "the Outfit," which was the organized criminal group founded by Al Capone.

In 1937, with the official backing of the Chicago Mob, Mickey relocated to Los Angeles to try and organize the rackets there. From that point on, Mickey's legitimate business and criminal rackets were everywhere in Los Angeles.

He operated legitimate jewelry stores, ice-cream trucks, dinner clubs and loan-sharking operations. He shook down and took money from local business labor groups and allegedly was at the center of a pornography and blackmail ring that penetrated deep into the heart of the Hollywood community and local government leadership.

He was credited by Meyer Lansky with helping to engineer the original partnership between the Teamsters Union and the Mob. He had the full support of Lucky Luciano to be the boss of the Los Angeles rackets and he called the famous singer Frank Sinatra a close friend. He was already famous (or infamous) after his testimony before the Kefauver government investigation committee and for his high profile and lifestyle in the Los Angeles area.

Cohen was a guest on a television interview

with Mike Wallace, where he became famous for his verbal attack on the Los Angeles Police Chief William Parker.

Mickey continued to stay in the local headlines, as he would operate legitimate and other, questionable businesses throughout his lifetime. He was diagnosed with stomach cancer after he left his second stay in federal prison in 1972. He died peacefully at home and in his sleep in 1976.

§

William H. Parker, Chief of Police
Born January 21, 1905
Died July 14, 1966
Los Angeles Police Department Chief of Police from 1950 to 1966.

Chief Parker was famous for hiring retired Marines as drill instructors and working policemen as he began his lifetime attack on the very large criminal population located in Los Angeles, California. He embraced and promoted a new policing philosophy of going after crime and criminals within the city limits.

The previous police chiefs had turned a blind eye to organized crime in the city, and as a result Los Angeles became known as Little Chicago, with all its crime-filled locations.

After Parker's death in 1966, Daryl Gates, his protegé, took over as chief of the Los Angeles Police Department and continued doing things exactly as Chief Parker had done. Both chiefs had their men out on the streets arresting suspects before crimes were enacted and throwing them physically out of the city with threats of great bodily harm if they returned. Organized crime in the city of Los Angeles just about stopped completely under the administration of both men.

Parker originally wanted to be an attorney, and he studied at several local colleges. He joined the Los Angeles Police Department while he continued his studies.

When Parker became a police officer, he continued his legal studies and used his knowlegde of the law as he attacked the crime in his city with proper procedures. He put together the famous vice squad called the "Gangster Squad," which would shoot suspected gang members without good cause, whereupon Parker would have the shooting justified in the local courts.

This led to fear in the crime-filled city streets, and most of the "bad guys" fled the city and went elsewhere.

Parker kept a close eye on the goings-on behind the scenes at most of the Hollywood studios, and many movie stars and executives were labeled, correctly or not, as part of the organized crime that was big in the area.

Parker served on the Los Angeles County civil defense council during the Cuban missile crisis in the early 1960s.

He died of a fatal heart attack on May 16, 1966, after attending a dinner where he was honored and received several commendations.

Side note: *Star Trek* television series creator Gene Roddenberry, a former Los Angeles police officer, wrote Chief Parker's press releases and speeches for speaking engagements.

It is said that Roddenberry modeled the character of Mr. Spock for *Star Trek* after Chief Parker.

CHAPTER FIFTY-FOUR

Charlie read and re-read the special notes that were attached to Police Chief Parker's file. It was the standard by which the Chief hired his special group of men who would go on to become the famous Gangster Squad that he organized to clean up L.A. from the gang members who were running wild in the streets.

Charlie had made up his mind to do the same type of clean-up of the underworld operating under their local leader Leonardo da Vinci, who was now in hiding somewhere nearby.

Chief Parker's words rang loud and clear in Charlie's head as he realized that he held the same special values as the chief had those many years ago.

The Chief's notes that Charlie copied down for his own use were clear and simple.

> Missions have changed over the years, but what has remained constant since the writing of the United States Constitution is law enforcement's commitment to protecting the lives of our citizens and the interests of our great nation.
>
> Our policemen have come to us from all walks of life to defend our city's ways of doing things and to prove that they have what it takes to protect, to preserve and to defend that way of life.

With these bold words encouraging him, Charlie put the word out that he was looking to hire special deputies for the Sheriff's Department who would be highly trained to enforce the law and rid the streets of lawless and criminal actions.

He turned his attention for this recruitment to the United States Marine Corps, which had a history and a great record of serving valiantly in every one of our nation's conflicts. He knew that for hundreds of years, Marines had fought, lived and died with honor to continue the legacy of their services to their fellow citizens.

Charlie, with Joe Wahl, made a formal call upon the headquarters of the United States Marine Corps in Washington, D.C. As a result of the meetings that he had with senior officers in the Marine Corp., the call went out to all recently retired Marines who would be interested in a full-time job as police officers, in and around the city of Los Angeles. The requirements were an honorable discharge from the Marine Corps, and each individual had to have had several years of experiences in law enforcement in the Military Police Division.

The response they received was somewhat overwhelming.

Charlie worked with Roberto Sanchez, who had a great deal of experience when he helped reorganize the SWAT teams for the Sheriff's Department, and they finally narrowed down the selection of this newly forming elite unit to one hundred and fifty men. Since these were already highly trained professional law enforcement officers for the Marine Corp., it only took six weeks to give them an understanding of the ins and outs of California law as it applied to the city of Los Angeles and its surrounding smaller cities.

These former marines were already in top physical condition and needed no basic training in hand-to-hand fighting or weapons use. Their time was spent getting themselves organized with the usual chain of command, which went from Charlie as the overall top commander, followed by Roberto Sanchez and then broken down into six separate squads of twenty-five men each.

It was late in June when Charlie was speaking to the newly sworn-in law-enforcement officers who were ready to make their patrols of the city on foot and on bicycles. It was thought that if they were put into patrol cars, they would not be able to interact with the citizens as well.

They were not to be on duty as were the regular Sheriff's deputies, who had their regular patrol duties. Their job was to get into the areas from where the Organization/Mob was operating. The ultimate goal was to find, locate and destroy Leonardo da Vinci XVIII and his gangland associates, and how they did it would not be looked at. They were to get out there and clean up the streets of Los Angeles from whatever gang influence they came across, with da Vinci as the prize, alive or dead.

Charlie gave the final and official speech to the graduating class, which had as attending guests the mayor, the remaining city councilmen, the press, and Sweetpea, who was escorted by Joe Wahl.

Starting tomorrow morning, the squads, who had the new name of "Gang Busters," would be turned loose upon the streets of L.A.

An excited Charlie kept his message short and to the point.

§

"Welcome, special guests and graduating sheriff's deputies.

"Los Angeles, California is one of the largest metropolitan areas in the entire country. We are the second largest city in population behind New York City. We have our own port in the San Pedro area, and several active airports located within our midst.

"We are in close proximity to the Mexican drug trade, home to the entertainment industry, and we have as residents, citizens who are incredibly ethnically diverse. We have all this, and everything works well, but we also do have a cancer that needs to be removed if we, as a city, are to maintain our general health. Due to these and a combination of other factors, Los Angeles has a colorful history of crime, including organized criminal activity, gang wars, riots and more.

"Although Los Angeles is generally acknowledged as a high-crime city, Mafia-related crimes have only a fraction of the foothold here that they do in other cities like New York and Chicago. Having started to gain their presence here in our city during Prohibition and peaking here in the 1980s, Cosa Nostra, the Mafia, spread itself throughout Southern California and has become the most prevalent crime organization in our city.

"Due to mob violence here in the 1980s, our homicide rate is leading the entire country. This high level of crime is attributed to the rise of crack cocaine use and distribution by the gangs under the leadership of Leonardo da Vinci XVIII, who is our major target. da Vinci is hiding somewhere in our city, and it is our job to root out this evil person and his organization, so that we can live in a quiet and crimeless city once again. A famous person once said that if you cut off the head of a snake, the body will die. When we get him, life in the city will be much simpler, and we will only have to deal with the local gangs, simple muggings, and a much-improved crime rate.

"In order to bring our city back to a law-abiding place once more, I charge you to find this man, and in so doing to clean out any and all of his organizational parts that you come across. You will be acting as heroes, and we shall all be standing behind you, cheering you on.

"Good luck to you all, God bless you all and the United States of America.

"Thank you."

CHAPTER FIFTY-FIVE

When Charlie reached the Sheriff's Central Station Headquarters the next morning, twelve of the most enormous policemen were waiting for his arrival. The size of them all was simply overwhelming, and he was very pleased. It was an over-whelming presence that he was looking for in his newly formed policing force.

Charlie introduced himself, his number two Joe Wahl, and Roberto Sanchez, the head of SWAT. He told them that the deal that he was prepared to offer the men who decided to join his newly formed group was that they would get special commendations on their records that would help them climb up the ladder of leadership for the Sheriff's Department. It was like getting extra credit for doing something special in high school or college.

Those who joined up would continue to be listed on the normal Sheriff's roster at the top pay grade, and they would be scattered as assigned to different stations within the city as their home bases, even though they would not physically be there for anything other than roll calls.

This new unit would not make arrests. It would be their job to intimidate and scare the shit out of the bad guys and also to smooth out relations with the good citizens of the area. If they had to book someone, they would call their normally assigned Sheriff's station and have someone come out and do the actual arrest and booking. They would have plenty of cash at their disposal from the government's Secret Service Fund to pay informants who might be helpful toward locating the whereabouts of the hideout of Leonardo da Vinci XVIII and his top gangland associates.

He explained that all twelve of the former Marines now present in the room were the top pick from over one hundred twenty-seven files that he personally read. He took some basic questions and gave answers to the best of his ability, and extended his invitation for an answer to the offer being made, directly to him, whether it was affirmative or negative.

§

When the time limit for an answer had run out, and he had finally talked personally to all twelve of the Marines, he found only four of them who seemed eager to sign up. The number four worked for him well with Roberto Sanchez from SWAT, who was going to be placed in charge of the new unit, thereby taking the total manpower number to five, which was the ideal number for a self-sufficient investigating unit.

Roberto Sanchez had immediately volunteered to lead the group, and Charlie noted to himself and to his private file on his investigation into his search for the Sheriff's Department mole that Joe Wahl said nothing. Again Charlie had to ask himself another unanswerable question. If Joe Wahl was really the mole that Charlie was looking for, would he put himself out front and in the open with such a group as the "Gang Busters" that he was forming? Charlie knew that he was still very far away from working out the answer to this seemingly impossible situation.

Turning back to the new squad, Charlie knew that he wanted hard men to do the difficult and often thankless job of turning the criminals from New York and Chicago completely around and sending them back to where they came from. Charlie had told them all that he was looking for hard men tough men, honest and God-fearing men, who would be ready to kill if they had to for the families and citizens living in their city of greater Los Angeles.

Each would be carrying two special weapons that the regular Sheriff's deputies did not have with them, and they were a tommy gun and a set of brass knuckles.

Now a tommy gun, whose proper name is a Thompson Submachine Gun, is an American gun invented by John T. Thompson in 1918. The tommy gun came to fame during the Prohibition era where they were used by both criminals and law enforcement. The "Thompson" was favored by soldiers, criminals, police officers and civilians alike due to its large .45-caliber cartridge bullets, its accuracy, and its high-volume automatic fire. It had been used by the United States military forces from 1938 to 1971, when it was retired from use, and all extra Thompson Sub-Machine Guns went on sale to the public for purchase.

This weapon has been called "the gun that made the roaring twenties roar," and it was used in the infamous Chicago St. Valentine's Day massacre. The tommy gun was a great weapon that could easily intimidate anyone who saw it, but it was a very big and bulky thing to just carry around. The tommy-gun holding case was a beautiful thing. It was about three feet long, a foot wide and two feet deep with a long handle. It was easy to believe that someone was carrying this long, black case with a violin inside of it, and not a high-volume killing weapon instead.

§

Brass knuckles are also famous for this era. They are pieces of metal shaped to fit around the knuckles of a human hand. Despite their name, they are often made from other metals, plastics or carbon filters. They are designed to preserve and concentrate a punch's force by directing it across a smaller contact area. A blow from brass knuckles usually results in an increased likelihood of fracturing the victim's bones on impact.

The extended and rounded palm grip also spreads across the attacker's palm the counter-force that would otherwise be absorbed primarily by the attacker's own fingers.

§

Charlie was trying to copy the style of Chief Parker, who had been in charge of creating the first "Gangster Squad" and had used his powers well and had great success. It was a different time, but the same old place, and Charlie was hoping for the same great results but wanted to get there from a new angle and with a completely different approach.

He wanted to stress the simple fact that Los Angeles was not New York, nor was it Chicago or Cleveland. He needed to get the information out there that Los Angeles was not going to put up with this lawlessness any longer. He was putting the word out to the criminal gangs out there that if you wanted to stay alive, you had better get out of town and hightail it back to where you came from. He now had an enforcement detail under his command and he had instructed everyone to stop playing Mr. Nice Guy and lean on them—and lean on them HARD.

Charlie took out an advertisement in all of the local newspapers and magazines and it read like this:

> The sun goes down early in Los Angeles this time of year. And then it gets dark, mighty dark.
>
> Up in the hills on Mulholland Drive or Coldwater Canyon or Laurel Canyon, the only light that anyone who is not on the right side of the law will see will be the flash of our police officers' guns as we put our guns up to the ears of our unwelcome

guests and ship them back east either by train or in a pine box.

Be warned: we are coming after you and there will be no warning. You can either walk away now—or be carried away later. We suggest you listen to this suggestion. There will be no other.

CHAPTER FIFTY-SIX

And that became the new Charlie Glass signature: the gun in the ear and a few suggestive words both spoken and written.

They definitely got the word out.

§

The Los Angeles Sheriff's Department under its leading investigator Charlie Glass was giving fair notice of his intent to wage an "anything goes" all-out war to drive organized crime out of the city and send its representatives back to the East Coast where they had come from.

The new Gangster Squad with its Marine-hardened tough men was made up of men who met each other on street corners, slept with tommy guns under their beds, and were determined to turn things around. Under Charlie's direction, the new squad planted listening bugs in mobsters' bedrooms and took visiting hoodlums into the Hollywood hills for that "Special Personal Chat" he had referred to in his written article ... with a pistol to their ears.

For Charlie Glass, all that mattered was nailing the bad guys and cleaning up L.A. Criminals would no longer, in the city of Los Angeles, be able to make a mockery of law and order. The aftermath of their combined efforts against organized crime would hopefully shake up the mobs enough to cause them to pull out their representatives.

Charlie knew that the one person who would not leave the area on his own was da Vinci. Charlie was starting to get bits and pieces of private reports of persons having sighted da Vinci as he moved from one location to another. The information was being gathered up from interested citizens and small-time Mob guys who crossed the path of the new Sheriff's deputies who were showing themselves around town.

Charlie had divided the city into a simple grid with twenty-four sections to it, and each day all one hundred-plus men of the new Marine/Sheriff's deputies, in uniform, would make sure that they were seen in each part of the city's streets. If these newly appointed Sheriff/Marine rookies came across anything that looked like a lead into organized crime's fingers in someone else's pie, a call would be made to the five-man special outfit that was now being called "Charlie's Boys" or the "Gangster Squad, Part Two" and they would look into the incident.

It took many weeks until the neighborhoods began to feel comfortable with the Marine deputies in uniform and the "Gangster Squad" not in uniform but still making their presence known, as they all circulated around from one grid area to another. The local businesses and the people in the street were expressing good feelings to their just being around as they would watch and listen to the doings of the neighborhoods.

It was into the second month of the new program when something positive happened. In a lower economic area adjacent to nearby downtown Los Angeles, a specific complaint was called in to the Sheriff's switchboard, and the caller asked to speak to someone from the "gangster squad." This was the first live call up to that moment.

The caller stated his name and address for his business, which was a small grocery store that he called a "flea market" on the corner of 3rd and Alvarado Street.

It seems that two well-dressed Spanish speaking young men who appeared to be in their mid-twenties had approached a clerk at one of the check-out stands and had asked where the manager's office was. They were shown to his office and met Aldolpho, the manager, who was the one who later reported everything to the Sheriff's investigators. Aldolpho was threatened with physical violence and the destruction of his store if an amount of cash was not made available to these men on a weekly basis.

That day was a Thursday and they told him that they would be back the next Thursday, sometime in the morning after he opened up for business. The manager smiled at them and agreed to everything they asked for, and as soon as he saw them leave and get into their car and drive away, he called the special telephone number that was being spread all over the area to report when something like this happened.

Adolpho said that they did not look Italian, as the investigator had asked, but they appeared to be "gang-bangers" wearing good suits and represented themselves as collectors for the Mob that was working the area.

On the day of the appointment, SWAT commander Roberto Sanchez and two of the Gangster Squad members were casually walking around the store when they saw the two well-dressed hoods walk into the manager's office in the back of the store.

The two mobsters opened the door and entered the manager's office, and were surprised to see sitting at the desk one of the Gangster Squad members, with a big welcoming smile on his face and a huge pistol in his hand, as he told them both to please come in. Another squad member also held a pistol in his hand as he leaned casually against one of the side walls. Pushing up right behind the startled men were the two other plainclothes detectives, who along with Detective Sanchez stepped into the large office and closed the door behind them. All five of the newly formed gangster squad were there to enjoy their first encounter with the now visibly shaking criminals.

No words were spoken as they were carefully searched, and a gun, a pocket knife, some cash in two envelopes and their drivers' licenses were placed on the manager's desk. The two hoods were pushed onto two metal folding chairs and their hands were handcuffed behind their backs.

Detective Sanchez produced his badge and informed them in Spanish, of their right to remain silent and their right to an attorney at a later date, and he told them that they were now under arrest. Roberto took their names and addresses from their drivers' licenses and continued to fill out the report.

Silence again prevailed as one of the standing officers looked over the paperwork, nodded to the others and held the door open as the two Mob guys were led out of the door and into the open market on their way to the parking lot where an unmarked police van was parked and waiting.

The employees of the store, who had been told in advance by the manager about what the police were going to do, all stood and cheered as the two handcuffed gangsters walked across the market floor and then were pushed into the back of the waiting van. Everyone in the market was talking, and hopefully the word would be spread about what they were seeing.

Commander Sanchez signed the transportation order and watched as the four-man squad took off on their way to the downtown jail's holding area.

Upon arrival, the two suspects were uncuffed and left in two separate but adjacent holding cells as they waited and wondered just what was in store for them.

CHAPTER FIFTY-SEVEN

The time of year was late autumn and the Los Angeles area would soon see the sun beginning to fade behind the towering and most majestic of mountains.

At around the same time as the sun was setting in the western sky, the same four-man squad signed out the two gangsters, cuffed them again with their hand behind their backs, and placed them again in the back of the transportation van.

It was just getting dark outside, as the van with the six occupants pulled into the same flat outlet on Mullholland Drive where the two original double murders had taken place. The four deputies, still not talking, set up two folding chairs in the center of the dirt parking area. They then escorted the two handcuffed suspects to where they were, then pushed them down to sit on the chairs.

The two men could not help but stare out across the flat parking area and look at the beautiful lights going on all over the Los Angeles area as darkness began to take hold.

One of the four Sheriff's men stepped into the circle area and went up to the closest of the two seated men. "If I may have your attention, gentlemen, I will explain to you the new rules that have now gone into effect.

"First of all, I want to suggest that you both look at the beautiful lights that are calling to you out there from our beautiful Los Angeles area that lies just below us. I want you to especially look at the lights that are just at the edge of the drop-off, which is about thirty feet away from where you are now seated. It is a wonderful sight, is it not?

"You see, I have been thinking about how to make my point to you, and have decided that if I have you thrown off the edge of the cliff, and get you closer to the lights below, then you would be dead, and if you are dead you would be in no condition to tell your friends about what is going to happen to them if they do not listen to what I am asking you to tell them.

"My second thought was to blow your brains out with your own guns, which we brought with us. An interesting thing about your guns is that they have only your fingerprints on them. We have been wearing plastic gloves whenever we handled them, so whoever finds your bodies up here will assume that the two of you had a lovers' argument as you watched the beautiful lights below. It will be assumed that you killed each other, and that will be the end of you both.

"But again, if you are both dead, how will you get out what I want you to tell your friends? So instead of blowing your fucking heads off," he pulled back the safety on one of the guns as he was speaking, "I am going to send you both back to where you came from, with a message to everyone that you come in contact with. But first I want you to feel the cold and sweet contact of your gun as I point it into your ear."

There was a slight delay as the detective held it up in front of the attentive stare of the two handcuffed men, and then took the loaded pistol and wormed its way (painfully, of course) into the ear of the first punk until there were major groans coming from him, and then he did the same with the second.

Moments later he stepped back, and the two barely conscious men had buckets of water poured over them to bring them back to a semblence of alertness.

"Here is the final message, so hear it loud and clear. If I didn't need a messenger to deliver it, you motherfuckers would be dead meat right now. But we can't kill the messengers, can we?

"Take yourselves back to whatever hole you crawled out of this morning, and tell them that as of tomorrow morning, if myself or any of my men see you two, or anyone else, doing bad business here in L.A. we will track you down and shoot you right on the spot.

"Nod your heads if you understand what I just said. I really should blow the head off one of you guys and let the other tell your friends about what it was like, but I am feeling good this evening and I will let you both live, at least until I see you again—and then, as the saying goes, "your ass is grass."

"We are going to uncuff you in a few minutes and put you in the back of the van over there. It is the one that you both have come to love. We have the address from your drivers' licenses and will let you go there to spread the word about getting dropped off the mountain top or getting your head blown off by myself or my friends. I am sure that you understand what I am telling you.

"Thank you for your attention."

CHAPTER FIFTY-EIGHT

And the information started pouring into the Sheriff's Headquarters in unbelievable amounts. Charlie had to assign two full-time office workers to work their way thought all the calls and paper work.

This was happening because the public was excited to be living in a real-life drama that was playing out in their streets, in their homes, and in their businesses. It became a game of sorts where everyone was watching everyone else's back, and the results were wonderful for the law-abiding citizens of the city.

Quite often the hoods were followed from the places of business they visited, until they stopped somewhere else in the city as they moved along. The people who followed the hoods would then point them out to the responding police officers, and an arrest was made right on the spot, and the reporting citizen's name was taken and submitted to headquarters for a prize or cash or both that would be given to them as a reward for doing their civic duty. It was becoming a game and everyone was doing it, and having fun as they helped clean up the streets from the bad guys who still were roaming around.

And the big prize was for matching the picture of Leonardo da Vinci XVIII with someone they might possibly see in the street or in a store. The reward was $25,000 paid to the person who gave the Sheriff's Department the lead that would end up with da Vinci either captured or dead. It became an exciting time for the public and everyone was out there looking around.

Of course, there were many false sightings called in to the switchboard about da Vinci, but each and every one was followed up because all it would take would be one accurate lead to find him. Charlie even went so far as to publish a picture in every newspaper, shopping place and public transportation area in the city, and every poster that was hung up had the following words printed underneath, which read:

LEONARDO DA VINCI XVIII – WE ARE COMING FOR YOU – IT IS ONLY A MATTER OF TIME.

§

Days turned into nights and then into weeks, and finally about one month later, a call came into the Sheriff's Station with CODE RED stamped across the top.

It was rushed to Charlie's desk, who read it carefully and gave it to Sweetpea, who was now spending her days at a desk in the control area working on the da Vinci case.

Charlie stuck his head in Joe Wahl's office and yelled "Let's go!" and the two rushed out of the office area heading toward the parking lot. Charlie gave the Code Red paperwork to Sweetpea and yelled over his shoulder, "Set us up—all cars —it looks like the real thing!"

Sweetpea, who had been trained for when this would happen, calmly pulled out her procedure book and started making calls on a private line that could not be monitored by anyone other than SWAT, the Gang Busters, and the twenty-five specially trained former Marines who were eager to receive this "all-points instant dispatch letter."

Sheriff's uniformed and non-uniformed personnel were all dashing to their cars to respond to the area listed in the special all-points bulletin. Everyone had been waiting for this to happen and they all hoped it was not just another false alarm again.

The paperwork was short and sweet.

> Fugitive described as Leonardo da Vinci XVIII, sighted with at least ten companions at the P.O.P. Santa Monica Pier. Full response requested as the sighting has been verified by police spotter via helicopter.
>
> All responding officers are to be in full riot/ protective gear.
>
> Los Angeles Sheriff's Department to take lead with LAPD to act as backup.

> Chain of command:
> Sheriff's Detective Charlie Glass as primary.
> Sheriff's Detective Joe Wahl as second.
> Sheriff's Department SWAT Chief Roberto Sanchez as the overall field commander.
>
> Bomb squad and SWAT teams are required to be in full protective gear at all times due to explosive software noted in front of office at end of pier.

§

The area noted as P. O. P. Santa Monica Pier was listed in the Sheriff's location book as officially called Pacific Ocean Park. It opened for business in the year 1958 as an oceanfront amusement park that is located in a city area adjacent to Los Angeles called Santa Monica.

The amusement park is located on the end of the large freestanding Santa Monica Pier that projects directly out on the Pacific Ocean in the direction of nearby Catalina Island. It is the only amusement park on the west coast of the United States that is completely located on a pier. The park provides an unrestricted view of the Pacific Ocean from anywhere within the park.

There are a total of thirteen rides within the park, including the world's only solar-powered Ferris wheel. It has one world-famous rollercoaster that completely encircles the entire park.

CHAPTER FIFTY-NINE

A command post was set up by the ticket-booth area where the pier started out toward the ocean. An overwhelming show of force was accumulated there, with the Sheriff's Department, the LAPD, the SWAT team and members of the local Santa Monica Police all present and eager to get involved. The Fire Department was soon to arrive also.

A note was handed to Charlie from one of his field officers, who had a message for him from Central Control. It was from Sweetpea, who had received an incoming call at her office from Leonardo da Vinci. It asked if Charlie would please call him on his unlisted cellphone so that they could talk things over before everything got unpleasant.

Charlie immediately called the number and heard da Vinci's loud, deep voice answering.

It was agreed that they would meet in the center of the pier at the merry-go-round, which da Vinci told him was always his favorite ride because it went around and around. They also agreed that they would each bring a second person with them, and da Vinci asked if Charlie would kindly bring him a large cup of coffee with two creams.

Charlie, who was loving the balls that this guy was showing, agreed to bring the coffee and said that it would take him a little bit of time getting it.

da Vinci, laughing, told him that there was no hurry, and that he had no other place to go. He would see Charlie and one other as they walked toward the merry-go-round meeting place.

They both agreed not to bring weapons with them.

As Charlie sent one of the policemen to get a cup of coffee with two creams, he went into the Sheriff's command trailer with Joe Wahl and Roberto Sanchez to talk things over. Charlie wanted to watch each man closely as they talked He was hoping one of the two would give himself away.

Once they were seated and all other persons were sent out of the trailer, they first agreed that Roberto's SWAT team leader, Ron Sellz, would accompany Charlie to the meeting. Ron Sellz was highly trained and could sense a set-up that could go wrong instantly. Charlie accepted the suggestion.

The three of them agreed that Charlie should offer da Vinci a peaceful surrender, hopefully with no one on either side getting hurt. They all said that they would go along with giving Da Vince a better surrender deal if he would talk about the organized crime set-up in the city.

It was Roberto Sanchez who surprised Charlie when he suggested that he place one of his best sharpshooters to keep da Vinci in sight just in case he was going to try something.

Charlie thought that Joe would have asked for the sharpshooter so that he could have da Vinci killed at his command when he could say that he saw da Vinci make a threatening move toward Charlie. Charlie was confused as he still did not know just who the mole was—and none of this was helpful.

The coffee with two creams arrived along with officer Ron Sellz, and the three men shook hands, and Ron Sellz and Charlie Glass once again put their lives on the line as they walked toward the merry-go-round in the distance. The normal night lights were on all over the pier area, and walking toward the merry-go-round was not a problem.

With coffee in hand Charlie and Ron Sellz stood there as Leonardo da Vinci and another nameless man stepped out of the shadows and into the light where they all looked at each other.

Charlie made the first move, which was to hand over the cup of coffee that he was holding, and he received a polite thank-you.

Charlie took his time as he looked over at Leonardo da Vinci XVIII and found him to still be a tall, dark and very handsome man, who seemed comfortable just standing there sipping at his coffee. It was very interesting to Charlie how da Vinci could look so elegant and relaxed when he must realize that he was a hunted man, and that his world of created fear, crime and hustling for a living was crumbling all around him.

It was da Vinci's suggestion that he and Charlie walk over to the standing merry-go-round and sit and talk things over. Each of them asked their seconds to stand by, and quite pleasantly, side by side, they calmly walked over to the merry-go-round, where they each selected a horse to sit sidesaddle on.

Charlie just knew in his gut that da Vinci would choose a horse that was higher up in its frozen position, and would indicate one which was somewhat lower for Charlie to sit on. Charlie smiled to himself. This guy was still role-playing and always seemed to like being the "higher up."

Charlie did not care either way and just took his saddle seat and waited for da Vinci to open up the conversation. As da Vinci had said earlier, there was no hurry.

"Charlie Glass is an interesting name for a policeman," da Vinci began. "It is a name that one can see through." He smiled his great smile at his own humor. "I have heard from my sources that you have been searching for me and the mole that you think is in your ranks, and I believe that I can help you with that, since your mole is my mole, so to speak.

"I find it most interesting how you have turned loose your new 'Gangster Squad' against me and made the good citizens of Los

Angeles eager to turn in my collectors.

"I absolutely do agree with you that it is time for organized crime to remove ourselves out of your city for a while. We can always come back at a later date when the people won't be so happy with the police as they are now.

"So here is my proposal. You arrest me and my men and make a big showing out of it. Who knows; maybe I can be of help getting you elected as Sheriff of your fair city.

"You charge us and escort us to the state line and make a big deal of it all, and in return I will, on that last day that we will ever see each other, whisper in your ear the name of the person who was working with your Captain Crewe for many years while he was helping my organization at the same time. And by the way, I really liked your gun to the ear campaign that you did a while back. It really got everybody talking about you.

"So, I give you your mole with proof of who he is, and you let my men and me go. Does this sound like a workable compromise to you? Putting me in jail does nothing to help you, and getting out of town will give me a new place to travel. We have a win-win situation if you will agree."

Charlie looked at da Vinci for a few moments, stood up and walked back to where his back-up man, Ron Sellz, and the second guy with da Vinci was standing.

Charlie knew that he was going to take the deal. There was really no downside for himself, and getting rid of the mole that was driving him crazy would be wonderful. He would be happy to let da Vinci get out of town and bother someone else. This would be some sort of a twisted justice thing after all.

He walked over to where da Vinci and his backup guy were standing, and put out his hand for da Vinci to shake, when a shot rang out and da Vinci crumpled to the ground with a perfectly round hole in the very center of his forehead. It was located just where a sharpshooter would center his shot.

As da Vinci collapsed, the blood from the wound splattered all over and covered Charlie from head to foot.

Charlie was in shock. Did the sharpshooter think that when da Vinci was putting out his hand to shake Charlie's hand on the agreement, that he had a knife or was attacking Charlie, and to defend the detective he had launched the shot in defense of him?

Charlie would never know, as he just stood there and looked down at the now lifeless body of Leonardo da Vinci XVIII bleeding out in front of him and the merry-go-round.

§

Three days had passed quickly and Charlie finally had a bit of peace and quiet as he sat at his desk and kept going over the events of the past few days.

He was being called a hero for removing the threat that da Vinci and his criminal Organization cast over the Los Angeles area. The Mayor and the remaining City Council members had authorized a special award event to present Charlie with a medal of honor for having cleaned up the city.

This was wonderful, and Charlie appreciated all the things happening around him, but, as he told Sweetpea, da Vinci's death stopped the discovery of who the mole was.

When Charlie had talked with the sharpshooter who had fired that deadly bullet, the soldier had told him that his orders were to keep his rifle aimed at da Vinci at all times. He was well trained and never would have taken that one deadly shot if he was not ordered to do so.

Who gave that order will never be known because both Joe Wahl and Roberto Sanchez were both standing behind him watching Charlie as he was talking with da Vinci. With all the noise and activity going on around them, the concentrating shooter heard a command that came from right behind him. "SHOOT!

SHOOT NOW."

Within moments of the deadly shot being fired, everyone rushed forward to aid Charlie if he needed it, and the shooter could not tell who it was that said those deadly words.

When the board of inquiry briefly looked into the matter, both Joe Wahl and Roberto Sanchez denied giving the order, and with the confusion that was going on at that moment in time, no one other that the shooter heard those words spoken, and the matter was closed, with great relief on everyone's part. da Vinci and the Mob were now gone from the city and everyone was pleased.

Everyone except Charlie, because the solution to his problem with the mole was still ongoing.

Both Joe and Roberto seemed pleased that everything was coming to an end and that Charlie remained unhurt. But for Charlie, nothing really was resolved. The mole lived on and he had yet to figure out who it was.

With the two lead detectives still working with him, Charlie felt that he was personally involved in a classic the-lady-or-the-tiger scenario that had taken up his interest in a college course he took in his rookie year as a Sheriff's deputy. The lady or the tiger? is a classical situation that definitely applied to Charlie and his frustrating problem.

"The Lady or the Tiger?" is a famous short story that was first published in 1882, and Charlie remembered every single word of it. The story had entered the English language as a person's problem with a situation that is not solvable.

The short story takes place in a land ruled by a semi-barbaric king who had some very progressive ideas, and some other thoughts that would cause people to suffer. The most famous of the king's ideas was to create a public arena to use a trial by ordeal as his justice system. The person's crime would be judged for punishment or innocence as decided by the rule of chance.

When the protagonist of the story was accused of a crime, his future was to be judged in the public arena where he would be made to stand before two closed doors.

Behind one door was a young lady who the king had deemed a good match for the accused. Behind the other was a fierce and very hungry tiger!

The accused was compelled to select one of the two doors. If he chose the door with the lady behind it, he would be found innocent and must immediately marry the lady. But if he choose the door with the tiger behind it, he of course was deemed guilty and was immediately devoured by the tiger.

Charlie knew that it was a simple story with an ending that would bring a particular problem to an end, one way or the other. The person was either innocent or guilty. End of discussion.

Charlie also had two doors behind which his two suspects were standing. One of them was innocent and one of them was not. It was Charlie that had to make the decision, and he hated having to do it without more information, and so he decided to do nothing about the mole until something came up that would give him away.

Until that time, Charlie went back to work.

TO BE CONTINUED